Song of
Immandra

MARIA COWEN

Chapter One

THE WARNING

The perfect azure sky belonged in a fairytale, as if it didn't know the menace threatening to overcome the realm of Sinead. Down below, the ageless trees seemed to be a little smarter than the heavens. Uneasy excitement trembled in the leaves and pine needles as the wind whispered its suspicions. The whole Dandelion Ridge seemed to undulate in the heat of the summer afternoon while the birds slumbered on the branches, waiting for the heat to subdue. The occasional chirp of impatience pierced the air.

Most humans appeared as oblivious to the heat as they did to the menace endangering their world. Immandra and Sian were not an exception. Perhaps it was the folly of youth, or better yet, their complete and utter distraction with one another.

The young couple ran down the grassy, emerald hill, happily laughing and holding hands. Copper glints reflected the sun in Immandra's dark hair. Her wide-set, indigo eyes and her pixie face indicated a mixture of fairy blood in her veins. Sian's hair, the color of ripe wheat, was just like the rest of the Reindeer Keep Village. He was taller than his friends, lean, but well-muscled. His large blue eyes matched the color of the sky.

Immandra stumbled and dropped to the ground among the tall grasses and wild flowers, pulling Sian with her. They tumbled down the hill, laughing. Sian protectively extended his arms around her shoulders and by the time their rolling path ended against a mossy boulder, they were in a tight embrace with their faces mere inches apart.

Immandra closed her eyes. Sian's face, so close to hers, made her head spin. She caught her breath as his lips descended to her mouth. It wasn't their first kiss, of course, but each time seemed to stop the elements and time itself.

And soon he will be forever mine...

The sharp crack of a broken branch startled them and restored the flow of time. Sian looked up with a slight annoyance. The ugly face of Kuiper Appleroot flashed amidst the branches. The gnome gave a knowing grin on his inhuman face, revealing he had been present in their company for a while. Kuiper only winked and disappeared in the green riot of leaves among the trees. Sian sighed with relief and returned to a more pleasant task. He kissed Immandra's parted lips again.

A furry, white face peeked out of the young woman's pocket. Roxy, Immandra's pet fae-fox, struggled out of the confining folds. Like all her kind, she was small, hardly larger than Immandra's palm. Her bushy tail made her look bigger than she truly was. Roxy shook free, looked at the love-struck couple, and rolled her eyes. The fox was more straightforward than Kuiper. She cleared her throat loudly. Sian looked up and waved at her to go away, but Roxy ignored him.

"It's time," Roxy announced with finality. She lingered nearby and waited for Immandra's acknowledgment, too stubborn to leave. "You'll be late."

Suddenly, Immandra snapped out of the enchantment of the closeness with Sian and remembered somebody was waiting for them both. The girl scrambled to her feet, trying to straighten her disheveled hair and skirt. Sian followed with a disappointed sigh. He gently removed the small pieces of grass and clover from Immandra's blouse.

"She's right. Let's go," Immandra said with a hint of regret in her voice. Her gaze lifted to the sky.

"Must we?"

"You know the custom. Would you rather wait another cycle of the moon to speak with him?" Immandra smiled.

"No. Of course not," he quickly assured her. He stroked his fingers around her ears to tidy away her hair. Both leaned in as if to kiss again, but Roxy loosed another irritated yip.

"Great sense of timing, Roxy," whispered Sian.

Roxy didn't allow Sian's acidic tone to bother her. She sprinted down the hill in long strides alongside her human friends. Their unique forms each cast elongated shadows beneath the impending sunset.

At dusk, the Reindeer Keep Village came alive with magic and whimsy. A gargantuan tree inhabited the center of the village, dominating the central plaza in a network of twisting branches that reached heavenward. Its lively essence cast a palpable presence, alluding to the sentience residing within its ancient trunk. Tiny wisps enjoyed weaving through the branches no matter the time of year or day, but they showed the most activity at sunset. Small blips in multiple colors shined and danced through the treetop.

Immandra's chest heaved and sweat beaded her brow, but nothing could delay her from wrapping her arms around the trunk of the beloved tree. Sian joined her in embracing the tree, still panting to recover his spent wind. Perspiration clung to his face and dampened his fair hair.

"You are here at last," rumbled a majestic voice from the arboreal depths. Every full moon, the great tree stirred and spoke, imparting wisdom and guidance on those who sought it. Custom dictated all speak with the Great Spirit before times of great change in their lives.

"Forgive us, Ancient One. We didn't mean to upset you," Immandra replied apologetically.

The hawoo tree had grown in Reindeer Keep Village for as long as anyone could remember. The oldest villagers said their grandparents' grandparents had played beneath the wide spreading branches, and many more generations before them. No one knew exactly how old the ancient tree was; only that he remained and spoke to all in times of joy and sorrow. It was said that only a dozen hawoo trees still grew and thrived in all of Sinead.

"Tell us, Grandfather, what our future holds for us. Give us your blessing," Sian requested respectfully. He chose to rest his own cheek to the cool bark, his eyes closed and ears open to the wise words.

"It is not you who upsets me, my children. It is only that... what I see in your future... It disturbs me greatly," the tree replied, his troubled voice ringing through their hearts as well as their ears.

"What do you mean?" Sian asked.

Immandra's worried gaze darted to her beloved, and she saw the same concern lurking within his youthful features. As she awaited clarification from the great tree, she allowed her fingers to stroke over its rough exterior in a soothing caress.

"I see tears... separation... Death lurks. Doom for all in our land. I cannot bear to look any longer."

"Surely you must be wrong. I mean no disrespect," Immandra replied warily. "But perhaps you tapped into a different source... a different time. Sinead is such a peaceful land."

Roxy twined around Immandra's ankles and quickly piped in her agreement. "Yeah, there must be some mistake." Her russet-tipped ears flattened back against her head in anxious worry.

The wind whispered between the sturdy branches of the venerable and cherished tree, rustling every leaf as if the Ancient One had shuddered. "I wish I was wrong. The signs are clear. Doom and destruction loom over Sinead. The inevitable approaches and it may be too late to thwart. I fear for the demise of many."

Sian and Immandra gazed at one another in concern. Slowly, the soothing stroke of her fingers ceased their movement and her hands fell away. Grandfather's words dampened her spirits and struck fear into her heart.

Above them, gauzy ribbons of cloud laced through the twilit sky, infinitely stretching toward darkness.

"Good luck to you, my children. May you have a happy future in spite of everything. Go forth with my blessing. Love one another. Take comfort in the present and cherish every moment."

"Thank you, Grandfather," Immandra graciously said. Despite his terrifying words of the future, he was owed the honor of gratitude. Sian echoed her sentiments and the couple moved away.

Immandra eased closer to Sian and welcomed the comforting weight of his arm around her slender waist. She gratefully leaned toward him as he led her away.

"What do you think it means?" she asked softly. "Sian, will this mean tonight--"

Sian touched a finger to her lips, silencing her words. "Imma, don't. Tonight... tonight will be perfect. Nothing will sway my mind."

"Speaking of..." Roxy tugged at Immandra's skirts with her teeth.

"Go," Sian laughed. "I will see you soon, Imma. I promise."

"Until tonight."

"Tonight."

***

Night fell over Reindeer Keep Village, but activity flourished. Outside, happy revelers toasted one another and animatedly chatted about current events, families, and the local gossip. Meat roasted over a fire, cooling pies lined a wooden table, and more villagers brought dishes to share for the festivities. Casks of mead and ale flowed freely.

Inside her home, Immandra sat perfectly still, listening to the sounds filtering in. Butterflies fluttered in her stomach and she sipped at a small glass of brambleberry wine in an effort to ease her nervous anxiety.

"No, no, no. Not *that* one. Use the silver and the white."

Behind her, two gnomes stood on a bench to work on her hair. They twisted and twirled the dark strands with silk ribbons into an intricate plaited style. Two pixies giggled softly while placing small blossoms in the finished braids.

For the hundredth time, Immandra smoothed her fingers down the skirt of her dress. The fabric exactly matched the color of her indigo eyes, carefully dyed by skilled hands. The top fit snugly to her slim body, laced at the back, and the skirt fell in a heavy drape to the ground. The toes of her black slippers barely peeked out.

"It is time."

Immandra lifted her gaze to the doorway and felt her heart swell with awe. The Fairy Queen herself stood in the doorway, radiant in her gown of shifting springtime hues. The immaculate, raven-haired beauty smiled and held out her golden hand. Immandra placed her own on the upturned palm and bowed her head.

"Thank you, Lady Sibba. Thank you for being here."

It was an honor to have the timeless and legendary Fairy Queen Sibba at her wedding. Immandra had never known her own parents, but she'd been told that her mother had been the child of one such creature. It had to be true. Immandra shared their graceful silhouette and sometimes seemed to have a mystical shimmer in her depthless indigo eyes. For as long as she could remember, she had been a dreamer.

As her mother had died birthing her, Immandra had been raised instead by her father's mother. Unfortunately, Grandmother was long deceased, succumbing to old age three years earlier. It greatly wounded her that Nan did not survive to see her walk on such a momentous occasion. It brought comfort to have Lady Sibba there in her stead.

Sibba ruled the fair folk of the forests with a kind and benevolent hand. Her kindness knew no limits. Many residents of Reindeer Keep Village believed that her nearby presence blessed their own township. In a way, it did. Reindeer Keep Village's close proximity with the fey meant that their protective magic overlapped with the human village. Immandra was only a quarter fairy at best, but she'd never been without their warmth and the knowledge of her ancestors.

"You look beautiful, Immandra. Just like your mother. I am sure she smiles down upon you this eve."

Moisture burned Immandra's eyes but she swiftly blinked it away. Tonight was not meant for tears of sorrow. "Thank you, Milady."

"Come, they await."

Lady Sibba led her from the house and down a winding path through the village. Strewn wildflowers bedecked the ground all along the way. Their sweet fragrance perfumed the air, strengthened each time a bloom was crushed underfoot. Smiling faces greeted Immandra as she passed. The village folk fell in behind her, creating a silent procession.

Dulcet tones from a strummed mandolin filled the night air, but the music could not drown out the low sound of chanting. The reed thin frame of Druid Thorn stood out against a fiery backdrop. In the center of the village, within sight of the hawoo tree, a large circle had been traced out on the cobblestones. Candles from every household made up the circle, in every color and standing at different heights. By custom, those who donated a candle carved a blessing into the wax for the couple's future. Joy, fertility, happiness, strength, and harmony were among the well wishes.

With each step Immandra took, her heart beat faster. She saw him.

There, on the far side of the flaming ring, she spotted her beloved Sian, led by the village warriors and hunters. Everything else ceased to exist, love and happiness blooming deep in her heart. Absently, she noted how Lady Sibba held up her dress as she stepped over the candles to cross within the circle, but all she could focus on was the feel of Sian's hands in her own. They were strong hands that always kept her safe.

Together they knelt down, fingers twined, while Druid Thorn intoned ancient evocations over their heads. The village elder cleared his throat and the excited murmurs of the crowd died down to silence. A hush fell over the many people gathered to celebrate the joining of two people.

"I call upon you, thou Great Spirit who inhabits all things. Fill this couple with your presence. Mother Earth, witness the union of their souls. By the Water of Life, by the Fire of Spirit, and by the all-pervading element of air, may your souls become as one. May you be bound by love as strong and as lasting as our land itself. From this moment on, you, Immandra of the Linden Clan, and you, Sian of the Stillwater family, are husband and wife. You may seal your union with a kiss."

His robust voice filled the air and spread over the crowd as a crashing wave. It moved them, to the depths of their souls, with each chanted word. At the apex of the druid's prayer, Sian and Immandra shared their first wedded kiss within an aura of golden light. The inviting presence rose up around them, enveloping the couple from head to toe until they became a beacon of jubilant, aurous color. The moment seemed to last forever until it became branded within Immandra's heart. She wove her fingers within Sian's fair hair and gleefully wished to never let go.

As the light dimmed and the flickering dance of the communal fire remained, the ceremony reached its conclusion, and the couple stepped from the circle with bright eyes. Tears glittered upon Immandra's face. Through blurred vision, she watched Lady Sibba's approach. Her serene features brought calm to Immandra's racing heart.

"A gift for you, my children." She extended both of her hands, in offering, to reveal the gleaming bands of two golden rings. Star emeralds shone from a dazzling setting, framed by ivy embellishments engraved in the fine metal. "If you press the ring to your heart and call for help when it is most needed, aid will come to you. It works only when your heart is truly filled with love. If you are angry, hateful, or full of fear, it'll be useless." An expression of concern crossed her beautiful face.

"Thank you, milady."

Lady Sibba folded Immandra's fingers over the gift. "I fear you will need it, child. I foresee… darkness embracing our land…" The beautiful fairy shook her head then flashed a smile down upon the pair of them. "No, not on your wedding night. Tonight let us dance and be merry."

Immandra looked into Sian's eyes and tightened her hold on his hand.

***

A cloaked figure made his way into the village. His dour appearance was at odds with the happy atmosphere, and those he passed shrank back from him. Several women called for their children and ushered them inside their homes or hid them behind their long skirts.

"Who invited *him* here?" an outraged villager demanded of her friend.

"Maybe he thought it was a funeral," the second village woman answered. "He loves funerals."

The duo made signs to ward off evil, exchanging doubtful expressions while clucking amongst themselves.

A third woman's speculative voice joined the gossip circle. "They say the genie lures young virgins to the Forbidden Mountain and--"

"Well, you don't have to worry about that, Mira," the first interrupted in a snappy retort.

The red-faced woman, a plump matron and mother to nearly a half dozen children, quickly hushed without uttering another word. She certainly wasn't a virgin anymore.

"He always brings bad luck, wherever he goes."

"Bad luck, bad luck."

The man ignored the scandalous chatter. He ignored their fearful looks and judging eyes. His dark gaze never left the newlywed couple and his gangly steps carried him to where they stood beneath the ancient tree. Kaitan Speedwell was a terrifying force to the humble villagers of Reindeer Keep Village. He had a reputation for delivering poor news and bad omens; using magic they believed was black sorcery. This was the darkest of spells.

"Beware! Beware! I see separation and tears for the two of you. I see storms rising on the horizon and destruction for all our land. Darkness is closing upon us!"

The guests stared at him, their faces reflecting a mixture of emotions. Some showed outright disbelief. Others, anger. Druid Thorn's face reflected only resignation.

"Omens or not, Kaitan Speedwell, this is a celebration."

"As if evil stops its plans for a party," Kaitan sneered. "You would do well to heed my words and ready yourselves."

"Enough!" Druid Thorn admonished. "Do not darken this bright night with your doom. Be gone from here, Kaitan Speedwell. You and your portents are not welcome."

The minstrel resumed the lively tune of his music, returning the attention to the joyous occasion. Soon, focus drifted from the man who raved and promised doom. Sian guided Immandra away, pulling her into the dance.

Tonight was their night.

***

The silhouette of a dark forest rushed beneath the wings of a crow in flight. Its black shadow hardly registered beneath the midnight canvas.

"Doom! Doom! Doom!" Its raucous cries echoed across the starlit sky. Below, the sharp-eyed bird picked out the gleam of many eyes. Fearful squeaks and angry chitters replied to the crow's warning call.

Forest gave way to empty sky and the reflection of dark waters. Ripples stirred across the lake, passing on the ominous message. "Doom! Doom! Doom!"

Kuiper Appleroot sat along the bank with his feet in the cool waters, a rough fishing pole in his gnarled hands. He looked up as the world around him hissed ominous threats of impending danger.

"Doom? What?" he scowled. "What kind of nonsense is this? Did the bride catch fire? The groom flee in fear of wedded bliss?"

"What indeed..." murmured the lake.

"We do not know. We must ask the crow," whispered the trees.

"Then ask her!" the little gnome demanded.

But the crow was already too far away, merely a speck against the moon. The trees rustled in the breeze and Kuiper harrumphed.

"Well, I don't think she knew, anyway. Crows tend to be rather ignorant. Although they have their moments from time to time," he grumbled as he retook his seat and plucked up his fishing pole.

Chapter Two

DARKNOOR

Dark warnings and prophecies of doom held no sway in their new home. The cozy dwelling sat on the edge of the village, with windows looking out over the green hills and flowering meadow. In the springtime, it would be a spectacular view.

Immandra stirred a pot over the stove and hummed with cheerful tones as she worked. The sweet scent of honey wafted upwards on fragrant steam from the cooking porridge. A bowl of cream and another of fresh-picked berries waited on the table beside a pot of cooling tea. A week after their wedding and she never tired of waking early to prepare her husband a morning meal. Tomorrow Sian would be required to return to his duties as a hunter, so Immandra intended to savor the final day of their honeymoon.

"Have I told you how beautiful you are?" Sian wrapped his arms around her from behind. He tugged her in close and nuzzled his whiskered face into the crook of her neck, pressing a loving kiss against her skin.

"Every day, my love, and I pray you will tell me so until we are old and turned into dust."

Sian lightly chuckled and delivered another kiss. "Age will never see your beauty wither in my eyes, Imma."

She turned and kissed him, arms squeezed around him tightly. When they broke apart, they both smiled and laughed softly.

"What shall we do today?"

"I'd thought a picnic," Immandra confessed, "but the weather this morning was damp and chill. More so than it should be for this time of year. No good for a lazy afternoon outdoors."

"Then an indoor one, only you and me. Roxy can have you back tomorrow."

Immandra laughed again and briefly turned her thoughts to her small, furry friend. Roxy had been her companion for as long as she could remember. The fox was staying with Druid Thorn and Immandra had no doubt the two would be ready and eager to part come morning. Roxy could be trying at times. Bossy.

Oh how I miss her...

Shaking away her thoughts, Immandra turned to gaze back to her husband. "That will be perfect. A picnic before the fire."

"C'mere." Sian tugged her to a chair while their food cooled in their bowls. "Your hair is like silk, Imma. I never tire of feeling it in my hands."

Immandra's eyes drifted shut. Every day she cooked

their breakfast, and every day Sian sat her down and brushed out her long hair. Calloused his hands might be, he weaved her hair into pretty braids with the skill of an artisan.

"Tell me your thoughts, Imma."

"I was only thinking how I'll miss our long days spent together. But also how I can't wait to see you at work in the village, casting smiles my way."

Sian chuckled. "What I do is not so interesting to watch."

"Maybe not the plucking bit, but watching you fletch arrows is beautiful to watch," she argued gently.

"I'd rather watch you at the looms."

Immandra worked with several other village women, spinning wool from their local flock of lambs. Her thread was said to be some of the finest.

"Listen to us," she laughed. Sian tied off the end of her braid and she turned to face him, pulling her husband down for a kiss. "We'll watch each other then, and hope we actually get our work done."

"I've always watched you, Imma. Always," he breathed against her lips.

Immandra forgot all about breakfast and lost herself in Sian's embrace.

***

Snow came early to Reindeer Keep Village, heralding the dark things to come. The downy white layer of fluff and gentle snowflakes laid a blanket upon the yellowed leaves littering the forest floor. Browned pine needles decayed beneath the powder drifts blowing in the frosty wind. Small animals kept to their homes and warrens, too frightened to brave the wintry world.

Druid Thorn stood at the village limits with his eyes lifted to the sky. A dozen dark shapes flew high overhead, though one peeled away and made a spiraling decent for the ground. He recognized the skinny bird, large enough to carry a man upon its back. The Mountain Fliers were a rugged people, all hard angles, gaunt faces, and lean bodies honed by strenuous activities.

The hooked talons of the bird dug into the frost-kissed soil, and the man atop the oversized avian tugged the reins. Struggling, the bird seemed to take offense to its master's control, but it eventually ceased its efforts.

"Do you bring news, stranger?" Druid Thorn slowly approached, mindful of the avian's sharp beak. It bobbed its head and studied him through one glassy brown eye, always appearing to keep the druid in focus. More villagers ventured out to watch from behind him, intrigued by the spectacle.

The rider bounded down and released his mount back to the sky. He offered a bow to the elder. "Yes, venerable one. I bring ill tidings and grave news."

"Come then and be our guest. Let us sit by the fire and warm our hearts with wine. When you are rested, you can tell us what brings you to our village."

Druid Thorn learned the man's name was Chappeewa. He led the rider to a communal hut where a fire burned bright and warm. As promised, he provided spiced wine, as well as a bowl of hearty stew. When the rider's breaths had evened and his limbs no longer quaked from the cold, the village elder asked him for the news.

"Mizar Thunderstone, known as Prince of Darkness, and his sister, Matta Dora, have challenged The Great Mother with their foul sorcery. Most disquieting rumors have been carried from Darknoor Castle, where they reign."

"I do not know these names," Druid Thorn confessed. "What do they exactly do...?"

"They steal the living essence which fills all creatures, and change it into a dark, evil, perverted force. Look into the fire. I will show you..."

Chappeewa set his curved pipe aside and dipped a hand into his pocket. He pulled out a handful of grayish-white powder and tossed it into the fire. The flames rose high, crackling in myriad hues of white and green. An image formed in the inferno, drawing the gaze of all in the room.

Two figures walked down a dim corridor. Torches on the wall cast flickering light over their shadowed forms.

"Souls are getting scarce around here." The man's voice sounded low, a caress against the ears in silken tones.

"So?" By comparison, his female companion had a voice sharp and chill as ice. "We will have to reach further then, won't we."

"Of course, dearest Matta. We'll double our searching team. Doom Fliers will have a chance to air their feathers."

"Foul smelling things," the woman muttered with a disdainful sniff.

"Oh come now. Since when does a little smell bother you?"

They passed through a doorway and travelled down a narrow, twisting stairwell. Dark cells with heavy iron bars lined the rough walls and rusty shackles hung from the beams overhead. They passed them without a blink, entering a torchlit chamber. A large brute of a man stood within, poking a sharp stick at three corpses hanging from above. He took a devilish sort of delight in the act, contorting his trollish features into an expression resembling a grin.

"This one is almost ready, Your Highnesses." The dungeon master's voice rumbled deep in his chest

The woman stepped forward, firelight shining on her silvered hair. Slender fingers, tipped by long scarlet nails, took the slack, upside down face into her hand to examine it with close scrutiny.

"Yes... His soul hangs from his body by a thin thread."

"Exactly as you like them, isn't it, sister?"

Matta Dora flexed the fingers of her other hand. With a savage thrust, she dug her claws into the dead man's solar plexus. Bones cracked and flesh squelched beneath her hand. Her fisted and bloodied grip withdrew, pulling with it a silvery cord of glowing essence. She dragged the victim's soul from his body, laughing softly as she made it dance in the air.

"Oh yes, this one will be delectable. Look how it struggles and quakes."

"Enough playing, Matta."

"You take all the fun from it, Mizar," she pouted. His hard look earned a roll of her eyes. "Fine then, I'll skip the fun bit."

The ethereal wisp drew closer at Matta's pull. Panic

and fear flickered across its ghostly visage, but there was no escape. Matta Dora opened her ruby painted mouth and inhaled deeply, drawing the soul within.

It disappeared down her throat in wisps of fading smoke.

Embers jumped and bounced within the blazing campfire. It cast flickers of warm and dancing shapes upon the concerned faces of Druid Thorn and Chappeewa. The small assembly of village elders joined them, exchanging worried glances and fearful looks.

"Matta Dora and Mizar Thunderstone bring great evil." Chappeewa waved the vision away with a sweep of his hand.

Shock etched deep grooves in Druid Thorn's wide brow. "They can't be permitted to continue with those practices!"

"She bathes in the blood of her victims and drinks their life's essence. Someone must stop her reign of terror! We must put an end to it for the sake of our people." Righteous indignation and anger seemed to overwhelm Chappeewa, twisting his hawk-like features into an infuriated grimace. He struck his pipe against the timbers of the fireplace.

Druid Thorn raised a hand. "Calm down, Chappeewa, calm down," he cautioned in a gentle voice. The soothing tones crawled with magical presence and invoked a sense of peace. "Nothing can be done if we lose our tempers. We need to plan this rationally. Matta Dora will be stopped, but it must be done with clear heads and calm minds."

Chappeewa slowly nodded his agreement. A serene

wind seemed to encompass the rousing group until the din of their frantic voices became a murmur. "You are correct, Druid Thorn. My apologies." He respectfully bowed his head, breathed deep, and continued. "Our elders went into a holy trance and it was then that our Old Mother spoke to them. She announced the time of Great Separation."

The whispers between the villagers promptly ceased.

"No," a woman gasped.

The Mountain Flier bowed his head solemnly. "It is so. The souls of all living creatures will withdraw deeper into the spirit realm, away from the world of flesh. What was one, until now, will be divided. The memory of oneness will be lost."

"The trees won't speak anymore? Waterfalls will not sing?" From across the circle, Sian spoke up for the first time. Pained disbelief echoed in his voice. "Birds and animals won't talk to people ever again?"

"It is far worse," Chappeewa told them. "Even human beings will forget who they really are. Concerned only with the needs of the flesh, they will slowly turn into beasts." Around him, the crowd gasped. "The heart of the earth will beat slower. The land will be covered with ice and darkness. It will be terrible! Terrible! Unless it is stopped…"

Druid Thorn's proud shoulders drooped under the heavy news. "Who will dare to oppose Princess of Darkness?"

Sian rose to his feet. "Something has to be done! You must call the rest of the village council, wise Thorn."

"Yes," the elder said. The druid straightened his

posture and gathered his strength with renewed vigor. "Yes. The bravest of our warriors shall go on a quest. We must find a means to thwart and destroy Matta Dora and Mizar Thunderstone. But to do this, we cannot act alone. Word must be sent to our sister villages and to the forest."

"I will send our fastest rider with word," someone called from the crowd.

Thorn bowed his head again. "And so it shall begin."

***

Immandra chopped vegetables upon the wooden cutting board, oblivious to the darkness lurking beyond their peaceful village. She let her hair remain loose around her shoulders, a silken sheet in a rich hue of dark red. Sian loved it best that way, and he also loved the emerald gown that was gifted to her by his youngest sister on their wedding day.

"Where could he be?" Immandra wondered aloud. With the hour grown late and the skies dark beyond the kitchen windows, she began to worry for her husband. Sian wasn't the sort to remain outdoors late, drinking and gallivanting with some of the other young men in the village. While she had delayed supper for Sian to return to a piping hot meal, she fretted when a glance through the windowpane revealed the meeting fires had dimmed. She saw a single man shoveling ash and dirt over the smoldering embers.

Sian had gone to the village meeting, led by Druid Thorn, to consider their plans for surviving the weeks ahead. Thinking back, she wondered if perhaps he had not gone to the meeting after all. Three times a week, Sian also joined a scouting party with the other men. They combed the surrounding area for game beasts to supplement their meager stock of preserved meats. She suspected her husband and the other hunters had encountered another difficult day of the hunt, as the deer were no longer numerous and the squirrels were gone to their winter slumber.

The early arrival of winter meant difficult times for one and all. Forced to harvest early to avoid losing the bulk of their produce to the frost, the villagers feared the possibility of a prolonged winter. A less-than-impressive stock of smoked game, dried beans, oats, and other grains became their communal stores. The fishermen, talented with navigating the ice of the frozen lake, took their chances on its thin surface, too fearless and determined to feed their kin.

Are things going poorly at the meeting? Immandra questioned quietly. With her brow knit in consternation, she pressed the knife blade through the carrot and resumed the rhythmic cutting pace. It was impossible to remain calm while the fate of the village was at stake.

Without warning, strong arms encircled Immandra's waist and chilly fingers settled over the bare skin below her three-quarter length sleeves. She shrieked and jumped, flailing with both limbs.

"It's only me, it's me!" Sian cried, leaping back. A thin line of red shone against his muscular left forearm where the knife contacted his skin.

"You scared me!" she fussed at him. She whirled, with the knife in her hand, to see Sian standing with both of his open palms raised and exposed to her. The frown didn't fade from her face. "I could have hurt you! I... I did hurt you!" Immandra tossed the knife aside and flew to him in a rush. She grasped his arm at the elbow and held it toward her for examination.

"I thought you heard me as I came through the door," Sian said. "Imma, please, it's only a scrape." He made a futile attempt to reclaim his arm from her possession, but worry made her strong as three men. She anchored the appendage at her level and frowned. It wouldn't require stitches or any sort of magic. The mild flesh wound required nothing more than a layer of healing ointment and a light bandage.

"No. I was lost in thought, my love." The rich smell of the burning juniper clung to his fair hair and clothing. "I'm sorry," she apologized, squeezing him tightly.

"It was my mistake for frightening you. But tell me of these thoughts. What worries you?" he asked her.

"Worry for you. And for the village," Immandra replied. She turned her face against Sian's neck, reluctantly pressing her warmer skin against his chilly flesh. He sighed in relief and hugged her close in an affectionate embrace. Kissing him was always best, but times came when she needed nothing more than a loving hug from her chosen mate. "What is the news of our winter rations? Will food be scarce?"

He did not answer immediately. The silence provided its own answer, feeding terror into Immandra's heart. Reindeer Keep Village had not known a shortage of food in years. In fact, so much time had passed that only the old-timers remembered the famine. Most of the villagers of Sian and Immandra's generation had never known the feeling of going to bed hungry. During those times, the young tried to sacrifice their food to feed the old and infirm. In turn, the elderly refused much of their rations when several young mothers reported their milk had gone dry. Suffering babes took priority over all, until a band of men traveled deep and far to barter for grain from distant lands.

It was happening all over again.

"It's more than that, Imma..."

"Sian... Tell me. What is wrong? What did you discuss?" Immandra asked, leaning back to gaze up at him. She cupped her palm against his cheek and gazed into his eyes. She saw only sorrow there, sorrow and shared worry for the fate of their people.

"We actually spoke very little of the food problems," Sian admitted quietly. "Mountain Fliers came bearing news of great importance, Imma. They brought a great and terrible tale to us."

Had the fliers brought news of greater importance than their projected food scarcity? Her bright eyes widened in alarm. Leaving the vegetable chopping for later, Immandra took Sian by the hand and led him to the rocking chair near the hearth. She fetched her first aid kit and tended to his wound in silence, once the dancing flames lit his pale features aglow with warmth.

"You needn't do that, Imma. It's barely a scratch," Sian assured her again as she knelt before him with his wounded forearm exposed. She extended over the arm of the rocker and bathed it in a cloth moistened with salve. He flinched, discomfort tightening his muscle until his veins stood prominent beneath his fair skin.

"Almost done," she assured him.

"I didn't complain."

Of course he didn't. Sian hadn't voiced a verbal complaint since their days as children. Not since the time when young boys and young girls began to feel the first stirrings of attraction and interest in the opposite sex. By then, everyone, but Sian and Immandra, realized they were destined for one another. She still remembered vehemently denying it when her grandmother broached the subject one fine summer evening. They were sitting on the porch, watching the youngsters kicking a leather ball back and forth across the village grounds. Boys and girls got along well together then, but Immandra and Sian were among the oldest of the village children. They fought like wildcats, friends one moment and avoiding each other the next. He picked on her for her slightly pointed ears, and she mercilessly teased him for being the shortest among their friends. Now he towered over them all.

That evening, Immandra chose not to play with her friends, sitting out to embroider a lace floral design for her new dress. She never missed a game. Her grandmother recognized the first signs of infatuation, the glances, the shy avoidance of eye contact, and she had teased Immandra gently by asking when the young neighbor gentleman would come to court her.

Seven years later, they lived together as husband and wife, happily living together under her deceased grandmother's roof. His family and the rest of the village offered to combine efforts to build the newly married couple a home large enough to raise a family, but Immandra graciously declined, eager to remain in the home of her birth. Instead, Sian, his brothers, and his father planned to knock down two walls and expand the home during the spring.

"You never complain when you're hurt," Immandra murmured, shaking her head. She closed the lid on the small box and stood, only for Sian to draw her into his lap. They comfortably fit together, but it was the first time that Immandra didn't receive comfort from the feeling of his unshaven cheek against her smooth skin.

Sian remained silent, radiating disquiet in palpable waves. She could never tell if their ring bonded their emotions, or if she had simply grown to know his mannerisms. Whatever it was, it knit her stomach into an anxious ball, nerves wound so tight she barely knew how to soothe him. "What is it, Sian. Let us speak now of it, love, or I will worry all the more for you and our village."

"The flier who came to us... he goes by the name Chappeewa," Sian slowly began, hesitantly. Immandra leaned back to read the reluctance in his features.

"Tell me. I am not a child to be sheltered from bad news."

"He spoke of the Princess of Darknoor. Matta Dora. He says she bathes in the blood of her enemies and raises an invincible army. Worse yet, that the Mother spoke to their elders and warned that the time of Great Separation approaches. If we do not do anything..."

"Then we will never speak to the birds and the animals again," Immandra finished.

All who dwelled in the world of Sinead knew of the fabled time of reckoning. A dreaded time so terrible that evil would overrun the world to blot out all things bright. Happiness would no longer exist, for the last of it would be consumed by the shadows. As old as time itself, the tale passed down from generation to generation. According to ancient lore, the long-deceased ancestor of the Fairy Queen Sibba first predicted and shared her cautious words with the humans.

And now it was soon to come true, if the Mountain Fliers were to be trusted.

"What do we do?" Immandra asked him. She curled her fingers into the fabric at his shoulders. Tears already stung her eyes at the very thought of losing all connection with the wilderness realm.

"We stand against her and fight. Druid Thorn will call together a war council, summoning the head of every house. I know Grandfather will answer, but I wish to be there. I want to volunteer to go."

"No," Immandra said swiftly. She shook her head. "I don't want you to leave. There are a dozen other men in this village who can go... and maybe half as many women capable of lifting a sword," she argued.

Sian's face fell and disappointment flickered across his features. "Do you not believe in me, Imma?"

She wrung her hands. "I do but... why you?" she whispered.

"How can I claim to deserve my place in Reindeer Keep Village when I let others step forward to protect it?" he asked her in return.

Immandra sighed and shook her head. Her cheek lowered to Sian's shoulder again while she held him tight. A vision bubbled to the front of her thoughts; their village besieged by hordes of Darknoor's fabled Doom Fliers. She envisioned the monstrous carrion birds swooping down upon them and shuddered.

"We were only married a few short weeks ago, Sian. I thought… we were to begin planning a family soon."

"We will," he assured her. "Fret not, Imma. The Great Mother guides us all in her own way, and she saw fit to warn us through the Mountain Fliers. Matta Dora can be stopped. Mother wouldn't give us an impossible task."

He's right. Mother would not forsake us now, Immandra realized, her heart flooded with relief. She swallowed the dry lump in her throat and nodded. Sian's lips became a gentle caress at her brow, his fingers sliding over her back. He soothed her and eventually her worries began to vanish.

"Tomorrow, Druid Thorn will call the war council and a decision will be made. Have no worries, my love. No harm will come to this village." An uneasy smile spread over his face, meant to comfort and relax her even further.

"And in the meantime?" she asked him.

"In the meantime…" His fragile smile widened into a mischievous grin. "In the meantime, we practice making a family."

She squealed as he swept her close to his body with one arm and rose from the chair. Supporting Immandra against him in a cradle, he strode to the modest bed, only a short distance from the roaring flames of the hearth. The humble dwelling inherited from her grandmother was tiny indeed, but suitable for a newlywed couple not yet blessed with children.

If Sian had his way about things, he and Immandra would not remain a childless couple for long.

Chapter Three

THE WAR COUNCIL

The morning dawned with gray skies under heavy clouds. Word spread across the village in record time, and what they received for their speedy efforts was a war council assembled from their most courageous fighters. Each of them sat beside a fellow member of the village, positioned in a circle with the Druid Thorn at its center. Their solemn faces stared at him, humans and a few sylvan from the local forest were among the number of heroic volunteers.

Druid Thorn appeared pleased with the turnout. With optimism in his heart, he raised his rattle toward the sky and beckoned the spirits to grant their blessing.

"We should all go to face them. We have a powerful enemy and it will take a great strength to overwhelm them. We can't afford to not give this our all," Dool Sarsall announced to the growing crowd. He led the warriors from the most prosperous family of Reindeer Keep Village. He stood ready in full battle armament, wearing his best blade and oiled cuirass. They barely seemed capable of containing his powerful muscles and battle-honed physique. It was as if the slightest flex might burst the straps of each armor piece.

Sian was one of the only men among the group wearing only his casual clothing. His grandfather had barely allowed him to attend the meeting at all, citing that his grandchild was far too young to become involved in the ways of war.

But he was ready. Sian felt nothing but grim determination when he considered everything at stake. He could not allow their village to fall to ruin, whether his grandfather believed him to be prepared for battle or not. With so many of the men willing to set their lives on the line to protect the village, how could he claim the right to love Immandra if he placed her safety in another warrior's hand?

"Then our path is clear," rumbled a thoughtful nomad as he leapt from astride his horse. The immense size of the beast and the man who rode it struck awe in the hearts of the many onlookers. "The Horsetails pledge our warriors. I challenge the Coltsfoots to do the same."

"No! Someone must stay behind to protect our village!" Serlig Coltsfoot cried in fervent disapproval. "If all of our warriors have gone to battle, what will become of those left behind? Our women and our children will be left defenseless. The Horsetails are hotheaded and rush into fights without thinking. It is a wonder they still live."

Sian laughed aloud at the counterargument to Furil Horsetail's boast, but he wisely bit his tongue and held back any agreement. The proud Horsetails had earned a reputation for their brash and reckless fighting spirit. As a clan, the nomadic people who roamed the lands just beyond Reindeer Keep Village distinguished themselves as some of the area's strongest fighters. They defended their people with unrivaled ferocity, but they were sorely lacking in subtlety and wit.

"Peace, I beg." Druid Thorn raised his hands and called for silence. "The danger is grave, but to leave any village without defense is folly. We must be wise and remember that we have little knowledge of Darknoor. Serlig Coltsfoot is correct to suggest we retain some of our warriors for the safety of the village."

"Aye," spoke the man to Sian's right. Willem Stillwater nodded his head, stoic features lined heavily with creases. His balding dome shone in the light, covered with a sparse layer of white and gray blended short hair. Once a warrior of the highest caliber, he was now reduced to bestowing his wisdom upon others. "A scouting party would be our best opportunity to assess the true depth of Darknoor's power."

"Agreed," the druid said. He folded his arms and gazed over the crowd of fighters. "We will need a small group of men—" A loud throat-clearing cough interrupted him. A single warrioress sat by her lonesome a small distance from their circle, spear in hand and braids swaying in the unforgiving winter wind. Her almond-shaped, brown eyes keenly stared at the druid. "And women," he finished lamely.

"Darknoor is no place for a woman!" Dool disagreed vehemently. "How could you possibly hope to stand against the forces of Matta Dora and her brother?"

The young woman grinned in the dwindling

firelight. "You speak the dangers of a woman to another woman. Are you daft? Or perhaps you have expended so much effort developing your overlarge muscles that you were incapable of strengthening your mind as well."

Enraged, Dool reached for his blade, but another fighter to his side quickly reached out to touch the warrior's wrist. The red-faced man quickly shook it off.

"Peace, please. There is no reason to fight amongst our own. A greater fight waits beyond the boundaries of our village. This is not the time to be divided!" the druid warned, raising his voice. "We are in need of capable fighters. It matters not if you are man or woman. Who among you will take the more dangerous road? Who will lead the way to Darknoor?"

Eager to prove himself, Dool stepped forward first. He refused to grace the young woman with even a glance. "I will fight. Who will go with me?"

"The Horsetails stand with you." The stern-faced nomad called Furil rose to his feet. "We will provide our strongest mounts."

"As will I," the young brunette offered. She pressed the end of her blade staff into the ground and bowed. Her long braids nearly touched the snowy ground. "I am Junua Cloudwhisper, a daughter from the Mistresses of the Storm. Matta Dora abuses her gifts and I seek to bring her to justice."

A low murmur of excited voices spread over the crowd. The Stormcallers were an impressive coven of witches who lived in seclusion. As fervent lovers of the Great Mother, they believed all magic originated from her, and they sought to punish those who wrongfully abused it. Matta Dora's number was finally up.

"I will fight in the name of all sylvan. You will find none more capable in the forests than I." Movement from the trees accompanied the sonorous voice. The creature who stepped forward resembled woody bark and vines in a humanoid shape. Elongated fingers tipped in sharp barbs were his only visible weapon, but they appeared to be enough.

"Yorteze Devil's Claw, you honor us." Druid Thorn bowed his head. A few other sylvan creatures in the group murmured their approval. Not all among their kind were designed for battle or as capable in a fight.

Serlig Coltsfoot and his brother Giber rose to their feet. "We'll go," Serlig proclaimed. "Someone has to show those Horsetails how to fight."

"We are as brave as they, only smarter," his twin Giber added. The identical siblings grinned at each other much to the glowering disapproval of Furil Horsetail. "Without us, the expedition would perish before we reached the hills of Darknoor."

The mighty stone-carved citadel of Darknoor held horrors unlike anything their group could ever imagine. Gargoyles, ravenous beasts, and angry soldiers awaited them. For each man volunteering to travel to his potential doom, dozens of men awaited in the opposing force. They had no true method to estimate the number of soldiers beholden to Matta Dora. Their scouting party was pure necessity.

"Six volunteers. Do we have anyone else?" the Druid asked.

"I shall go," Sian said proudly. "For the Stillwaters."

"No, he is too young," Grandfather Stillwater spoke up swiftly in angry disapproval. His disagreement gave

Druid Thorn a reason to pause. Sian's family patriarch settled back and shook his head.

"I am as brave as any warrior here!" Sian argued. "It is my right to defend our people against this threat." The youngest Stillwater puffed out his chest defiantly. He wanted to prove himself and earn the respect of his family, but most of all, he wanted to help safeguard the village from evil.

"Do my words mean nothing to you, Sian? Think of your young wife and the rest of our family. If I was a younger man, I would fight. If your father were still among us, he would gladly go, but you are the last male heir of age in our clan. Rethink this."

"For what reason do you ask him to stay behind?" Druid Thorn asked.

"Druid Thorn--" Willem spoke respectfully, "My grandson is youngest among us and ill-prepared. He has never faced war or hardship such as this. He is not ready."

"That is all the more reason to go, Grandfather. If this adventure party fails on the road, the battle will come home. Our line will only end here in Reindeer Keep Village instead," he spoke hastily.

Willem sighed deeply and puffed his pipe. A hush of silence fell over the council like a crashing wave, until only the sound of crackling twigs and firewood filled the air. "Have you spoken of this with Immandra?"

"I have. She gives her blessing."

Druid Thorn offered an encouraging smile to the brave youth. "If that's settled, let us return to the business at hand."

"There is danger regardless of where the lad chooses

to fight," Furil Horsetail muttered scornfully. "If we are unsuccessful in our mission, all is as he says. He may very well perish in your village."

"He has my blessing," Willem agreed reluctantly.

The Druid elder gazed at the pair of Stillwater men and nodded his head. "So be it. This will be your trial, Sian. The seven of you are to travel to Darknoor. Along the way, you will gather news of this threat and return word to us by messenger. Notify all villages along the way. Chappeewa promises to do the same. The rest of our people will prepare for attack."

Sian's body felt flushed with nervous excitement. He rubbed his hands together and stole a glance at the worried features of his grandfather. Why couldn't he understand how necessary it was for them all to make sacrifices? Sian didn't choose the path of battle for glory, but because it was necessary. Many of the other village men were long past their prime and no longer fit for battle. The others of his age group lacked his skill with a blade.

"What of the fairies?" a woman called from the crowd. "Will they not send aid against Darknoor?"

A frown tugged Druid Thorn's face down into a somber expression. "Queen Sibba sends word. With the strength of winter upon us, their powers wane. They can do nothing to aid against Darknoor."

Protests arose but the elder lifted his hands, calling for silence.

"They will not abandon us, good people," he appeased with gentle tones. "She has promised to send food if found and continue to do her best to shield our village from the full storm's brunt."

"Bah! Enough of the fairies then. They dance and sing, they do not fight," Dool said dismissively. "Chappeewa, what else can you tell us?"

"The road to Darknoor is riddled with dangers of all kinds. Unnatural creatures guard the castle and evil spells protect the walls." Chappeewa flattened the snow with a stroke of his palm and drew a rough illustration on its ivory surface. "Here is the way... It is most safe to travel between the moors and the plains. Any other path will be suicide," the rangy flier explained.

"The Doom Fliers are perhaps the worst of the perils awaiting you. They are my own people and our favored mounts, twisted into cruel aberrations against our will. We have lost countless many over the years."

"So it's true then? The tales?" Yorteze rumbled in his deep baritone.

"Aye, it is. For each of us who disappears from home, we know another has been pressed into the ranks of Matta Dora's army. With magic, a Mountain Flier's soul is spliced with the essence and body of his mount. It is a sinister act of sorcery. Irreversible. The only cure is death. If you should find the chance to dispatch a Doom Flier, do so. You do a kindness to the tortured soul within."

Sian suppressed the urge to shudder. He didn't want to risk the chance of his grandfather pleading for him to remain home again. Doom Fliers were known for eviscerating their victims and feasting upon the still warm entrails.

"This is the path you will follow. It is a harsh ride of a fortnight if you travel as the crow flies. There, you will encounter her fortress."

"What is it like?" Giber asked eagerly.

"A city taken hostage by a prison, with Matta Dora serving as the executioner," Chappeewa answered bluntly. "It is said a gentle countess once ruled the area, beloved and praised by her people. When famine fell upon them, she called upon the services of a sorceress to bless the land."

"But Matta Dora betrayed her," Junua said, nodding her head along to the story.

"Yes. She stole the throne for herself. She seduced the countess' generals, brought her brother to serve as governor of the people, and now they terrorize villages to perform their sick fantasies."

The Mountain Flier continued to draw another illustration. "Beyond the city gates, you will find merchants, homes, and innocents. I have no doubt that others have been swayed willingly to join her side. Many of my people have died to gain this information. We are at our limit. We can do no more."

"That is fine, Chappeewa. It is our turn to repay the favor and to help you in kind," Druid Thorn kindly said, clapping a hand to the lanky flier's shoulder.

Warriors leaned over his shoulder for a look. They divided the remaining hours after nightfall between constructing battle plans with the war council and seeking the comfort of their families. The men returned to their homes and loved ones, and once morning came, they awakened early to set out on their grand adventure.

"Please be safe," Immandra beseeched him. She tenderly held his face between her hands and kissed his lips while the other men saddled and prepared their mounts. They may have spent most of the night whispering quiet reaffirmations of their love for one another, but he knew in his heart that Immandra didn't wish for him to leave.

A soft, grass-scented nose nudged him from the rear. His stallion stood behind them, a tan and white pinto with an unruly ivory mane and soulful brown eyes. Immandra stroked the equine's brow and smoothed his white forelock.

"We'll be fine. Isn't that right, Emmer?" Sian asked the horse. The animal seemed to smile in his own way.

"It's time!" Serlig called from horseback. He and his brother sat astride their identical mounts. Both copper-red horses nickered and playfully nipped at one another in play. They tossed their strawberry blonde manes and stamped their hooves impatiently.

"I... suppose--"

Immandra kissed Sian again, interrupting his awkward farewell. "I will see you again soon. Promise me."

"I promise," Sian vowed to her. He leapt upon the saddle, lest the others become impatient with their tearful show. Leaving Immandra was the most difficult part. He'd already hugged his mother and each of his younger siblings, but this moment was for Immandra and her alone.

Within minutes, the seven armed warriors began to travel the path winding down from the village. Their friends, family, and fellow villagers stood at the edge of the forest to wave goodbye.

Immandra was not among them. Sian glanced back over a shoulder to see her lone form a distance away. Tears glistened in her eyes.

Chapter Four

THE PRINCESS OF DARKNESS

Gray clouds hung heavy over Darknoor, shrouding the sun's valiant attempt to cast its warm light over the land. The villagers trudged about the lower city on their daily tasks under the watchful eyes of black-clad guards. Most of the warriors were human, but others less so. Some had hulking figures with squashed faces, while others had a leaner look and sharply pointed teeth. The black of heart were drawn to Darknoor like moths to a flame and they gladly pledged their loyalties to Matta Dora and her rule.

"This bread is dry as a husk."

A roll sailed across the room and struck the wall with a dull thud. Two hounds snarled and gnashed their teeth at each other in a fight over the scraps. The soft bread easily tore apart beneath their attacks.

A rhythmic tapping accompanied the drumming of crimson painted nails on the table. Matta Dora's annoyed gesture made the whole staff cringe. The silence dragged for what seemed forever, only the staccato *tap, tap, tap, tap* filling the air.

Imbecilic fools. Sheep too scared to even fix the problem.

Matta Dora rose to her feet, provoking a wave of fearful reactions. The sight served a delicious thrill to the woman. She savored it as much as she despised their weak-willed cowardice.

"I will not have such slop gracing my table," she hissed.

"What seems to be the problem my dear Matta?"

Cool hands settled on her shoulders from behind, accompanying the deep voice that always acted as a balm to her anger. She leaned backwards into the touch.

"The baker dares to serve me a brick, brother."

His strong hands tensed, but in her mind's eye, visions of cool fury swept through her thoughts. More than once in the past, Matta Dora was witness to her brother's breathtaking anger and righteous indignation. She lived for it. Outrage suited Mizar's dark blue eyes, as did the furrow on his brow and the tightness to his jaw. It made him handsome.

"Shall I set an example for you, darling sister?" His husky voice whispered against her ear.

"I would like to do some scrying…" Matta twisted a silvery blonde curl around her finger and lifted her lips in a thoughtful smile. "Would you see the baker serves some use for me, brother?"

Mizar's chuckle sent a thrill through Matta's body. She turned and tilted her head back to aim a smile up at her taller brother. Like her, Mizar's hair shone silver in the light of the castle lamps. The flickering lights picked out the occasional golden glint from the shoulder length strands. Jeweled studs lined the length of his pointed ears.

"If a baker cannot provide the softest of breads, then there is not much use for her, hmmn?" Mizar tipped her chin upwards and pressed his cool lips to her brow. "I will see it done."

"I will go prepare." Matta Dora licked her lips in an eager fashion, eyes shining.

No one stepped in her way as she left for her chambers. Matta preferred her rooms in the upper reaches of the castle where she had an unbroken view of the surrounding lands. The misery of the people, she said, was her morning song. It was their quiet despair, her lullaby.

Sumptuous velvet curtains hung over the windows to block the sunlight from entering the room. Everything held a touch of opulence, from the silk sheets covering the bed to the decorative mosaic tiles patterned on the walls in a colorful, but grim mural.

Engraved in the smooth floors was a large pentacle, perfectly chiseled into the stone. Arcane glyphs in gold and silver surrounded the outer perimeter. Fat candles sat at each point of the star. It only took a wave of her hand to set all five alight. Red wax began to slowly drip down their sides.

While she waited, Matta started her preparations. She traded her decadent gown for a plain, silken robe and let her hair down from its intricate braids. Next, she dotted fragrant oils on her wrist and neck. The musky-sweet scent filled her nostrils with each deeply indrawn breath. A knock interrupted her quiet reverie, but instead of anger, Matta felt only anticipation. Outside the door, a servant knelt with a silver pitcher, held above her head, in supplication. Flour dusted her chestnut-brown hair and smudged her dull woolen dress. Matta's nose briefly wrinkled at the scent of burnt bread and sweat wafting up from the quivering girl.

"Don't repeat your mother's mistakes." Matta Dora laughed and plucked the pitcher from the baker's daughter then closed the door in the girl's face. *He must have made her watch. Oh to have seen her face then... Another time,* she promised herself. For now, she had her own work to do.

She poured the contents of the pitcher into a large, shallow bowl and then carried the latter with her to her place of magical workings. A stool sat in the direct center of the pentacle and Matta took her seat, placing the bowl on her lap. A smile curled her lips as she swirled the still warm liquid around and around with her finger.

"Show me what I wish to see. Cast my vision far and wide." When she lifted the slender digit away, an image began to form on its surface.

The Princess of Darkness suckled on her bloody finger and watched with growing interest. "Well, well... what have we here?"

The swirling shadows coalesced into a clear image of a bleak winter's day. Riders on horseback travelled across the hills and plains. They all bore weapons meant for battle. She counted six humans and a single sylvan, the latter making her smile widen.

"Fresh souls. This *is* a pleasant surprise"

She watched the images for an hour's time, her smile only widening when the group reached a village.

Instead of seeking shelter, she watched as they roused the people and brandished weapons. They spoke of uniting. They spoke of preparing themselves and standing together against a single threat known as Darknoor.

"A ragged bunch of peasants dare to play heroes, do they? This ought to be fun. I haven't had a challenge in quite some time. What a delightful distraction."

From her pocket, she drew a small silver bell. Its sharp chime summoned a servant within seconds. The boy bowed, trembling in his thin robes, and kept his eyes downcast. Matta tasted his fear and savored it as much as she enjoyed the panicked expression contorting his dirty face.

"Summon General Stern for me, boy. I want to send a message for these... heroes."

"At once, Your Highness." He dipped down further and then shuffled backwards to leave the room. No one turned their back on Matta Dora. No one.

She chuckled and tilted the bowl again to give it another swirl. She really did love playtime.

***

"How many do you think will fight?" Sian looked across to Dool and shaded his eyes from the sun's harsh glare. The light reflected off the snowy ground and made his head ache as if he stared too long.

"All of them, if they know what's good for them," the gruff warrior replied. "The three villages we passed pledged roughly thirty men each and they'll spread out to the villages east and west of our path. If all goes well, when we return from our scouting, we'll have at least two-hundred men."

"My clan had pledged our services. We're small, but it takes only a single witch to match the might of ten men."

Both Sian and Dool glanced back at the woman riding behind them. Despite Dool's initial apprehensions, Junua's presence garnered support from the village elders. Everyone knew tales regarding her coven. Hearing and seeing that the witches stood with them bolstered spirits.

"How many..." Sian ventured to ask. The brunette smiled back at him, her white teeth flashing in her dusky face.

"If we march on Darknoor, you will have the aid of five of my sisters. The rest will spread across the villages to stave off any attacks."

"Or work as a final line of defense," Door muttered. Junua merely nodded her head. "Anyway, the next town is the largest of the bunch, being near the forest--"

"Smoke!" Giber's shout cut off Dool. The group slowed and turned their heads toward the horizon. Thick, black plumes rose into the sky.

"The ground cries in pain," Yorteze relayed in a grave tone. "The forest is restless and the animals have all fled."

"An attack?" Giber's horse softly knickered and tossed its head. All the horses restlessly moved, spooked by the scent of fire and death drifting to them on the chill wind.

As one, the group urged their mounts into a run. The snowy ground raced past beneath them while clumps of dirtied slush kicked up in their wake. Ruin awaited them in the town. Every building and home smoked and was razed to the ground until it was hard to tell what they had ever been.

"Where are the people?" Serlig's quiet voice left his lips in a rush. "There aren't enough bodies."

"Spread out, we need to see if anyone still lives." Furil was the first to dismount and tether his horse. The others followed suit and then slowly ventured into the village remains.

Sian's stomach twisted into knots and his throat burned. His lunch threatened to come up, but he fought the sick feeling down and tried not to breathe through his nose. Charred wood and shattered pottery crunched beneath his booted feet.

"Over here!" Dool yelled.

The group rushed to his shout with their hands on their sheathed weapons. The found Dool crouched down next to a man caught beneath a broken well. Heavy rocks kept his body trapped.

"Go. Run!" the man gasped wetly. Blood trickled from the corner of his mouth.

"Easy. We're here to help." Dool rummaged for bandages in his pack while Junua tipped some water into the man's mouth from her waterskin.

"No. No help. Just run. Run before they take you too!" The man wheezed and began to cough. More blood foamed up from his throat.

"Who?"

"The Dark Princess sent her soldiers. They struck us at dawn. They took our women and children, some of our men too." The man coughed again, his movements growing weaker by the second. Junua caught Dool's eye and gave a small shake of her head.

Sian remained silent and grim, his hand fisting over the hilt of his sword. Anger heated his blood, but fear sent shivers down his spine. He glanced around at all the dead and couldn't decide which feeling held dominance.

"He is gone," Junua announced reverently. "May the stars guide his soul to rest and the Mother welcome him with open arms."

Everyone bowed their heads in a respectful moment of silence.

"We'll camp the night here," Furil said in his low voice. "To enter the forest at nightfall is folly."

"You want us to sleep among the dead?" Fear trembled through Giber's body and Sian could not blame him. The idea of sleeping near corpses made him uneasy too.

"No. We have a few hours yet. We will do our brethren the decency of a burial." Furil plucked a shovel from the debris-strewn ground. The charred handle appeared serviceable and he tossed it at the fidgeting brother. "Come. We'll all take turns digging."

The sun dipped below the horizon as the group patted the last mounds of dirt into place. With their brows sweaty and their muscles sore, everyone eagerly made up camp without complaint. Yorteze used his strength to fashion a windbreak using the stones that had once, formed homes and stores. Junua prepared a roaring fire to keep them warm and frighten away any scavengers who might be drawn to the destroyed town. They ate dinner, each one silent and lost to their own thoughts.

"I will take the first watch," Junua announced. As you dug, I circled the town. I found tracks leading into the forest. Many people were herded from this place."

"Just as the old man said." Dool sighed and threw another log into the fire. Sparks flew up in the air.

"We can't just leave them to be prisoners," Sian argued quietly.

"And what would you have us do, boy?" Furil stared across the flames at Sian. "We are seven and they are many. Our job is to scout and decipher their strengths. No rescues can be made without an army."

He's right, but it just feels so wrong. Sian sighed, but nodded his head. "I know. I'm sorry. It just makes me sick to think…"

"It makes us all sick, Sian." Dool patted his back. "Get some rest. You and I will take watch after Junua, then Giber and Serlig after that, and then Furil and Yorteze."

Sian stretched out on his bedroll and tried to turn his thoughts to happier things such as his family and his wife. *Oh Immandra, at least you are safe my love.*

Indigo eyes filled his dreams.

Chapter Five

THE VISIONS

Snowflakes danced in the sky, drifting downwards in slow and lazy spirals. The large puffs had steadily fallen since their warriors left, and Immandra worried it was a sign of coming times. The entire village was quiet, subdued with an uneasy air of anticipation.

In the center of the village, the ancient hawoo tree held a thick layer of snow on its spreading limbs. Glistening frost rimmed every leaf, its long and elegant branches burdened with ever-piling white powder. Immandra ducked beneath and found some small respite from the building storm. She brushed her gloved hand over the gnarled trunk to clear a patch of clinging ice, then pressed her rosy cheek to the rough bark.

"It's… it's been so long since Sian left. Nearly a month's time with no word from any of the scouts." It had been twice the time predicted to make the trip to Darknoor. The entire village was on edge, though no one dared to admit their worries aloud. "Grandfather I need you. There is no word, no news at all. Please tell me s-something," she pleaded on a sobbed breath.

The grandfatherly old tree remained silent for a time until Immandra feared he would offer no words of wisdom to her at all. Had he gone into the deep sleep as many of the other sylvan? Just as she nearly gave up hope, his creaky, ancient voice rumbled words of advice to lift the tremendous weight from Immandra's heart. "Come, come, little one. I wish I could help you, but I am only an old, wizened tree. The burden of centuries rests upon my branches. Go to the lake. Look upon the waters. Ask them," he advised wearily. "There you will find the answer you seek and a guide to light your path."

"Then I will go. Thank you, Grandfather," she whispered, kissing his cool bark.

Night fell and the moon rose high in the sky long before Immandra reached her destination. The lake's beauty had been untouched by winter, perhaps enhanced by the majestic rise of shimmering snow flawlessly bordering the body of water. She knelt at the edge of the ice and lowered her gaze to the dark surface. Still and peaceful midnight water glittered beneath the starlit night, reflecting the silver moon. She wished Sian were beside her in his scarf and mittens, sheltering her from the cold, with his strong arms around her.

"The hawoo tree sends me to you for guidance. Tell me, wise waters, did anything happen to Sian Stillwater? Please tell me," she pleaded gently. The water had always been the patron spirit of Sian's clan and their watchful guardian. She had to believe that it would not lead her astray.

Ripples of movement spread throughout the nearest

section of the lake, releasing the song of many voices with each swirling motion. "It is difficult for us to understand the affairs of man. Ask us about the fishes or the otters. Ask of us of the heron and goose. Would you like to know of the water creatures, dear one?"

"No, I need to know about my soulmate. Of Sian Stillwater, one of your very own. Please, peaceful waters, I know it is within your power to tell me more of his fate. Where is he now?" Immandra persisted.

A faint sigh escaped the babbling water. Immandra strained to hear the whispers beneath the hiss of the wind between the trees. "Sian... one favored among us. A gentle child. We will try..."

The water surface clouded like condensation fogging a translucent glass. Vague colors appeared to Immandra at first, but these quickly took shape and formed into people. She recognized the seven riders almost at once.

The warriors rode down a winding path, through a thick forest, with Door and Furil in the lead. Junua, riding bareback without a bit or reins, trailed the rear of a beautiful copper mare. The horse simply seemed to understand the needs of her mistress, as if they were of one mind. Unlike the men, she seemed oblivious to the snowfall that speckled their clothes and hair with white, only to melt away.

Serlig and Giber Coltsfoot moved side by side on their matching geldings, chatting about the best way to behead a man. Sian followed behind them on Emmer, tunefully whistling the song played on his wedding night. Their sylvan companion travelled in patient silence, only a few paces ahead of the sorceress in their midst.

All appeared well.

The attack came without warning. Over a dozen men charged from the trees, seamlessly hidden in the shadows. Their swords flashed in the sharp winter light.

Yorteze Devil's Claw dropped the first enemy with a bolt to the man's chest. The projectile, formed from the same woody substance as his body, shot from the sylvan's open palm. It tore through armor and sank deeply, aimed for the heart.

Furil yelled out in a savage cry and thundered forward on his mount, crashing through the enemy ranks. He pulled out his bow and let loose with an arrow, placing two feathered shafts into an enemy's back before he was pulled down from his horse and forced to melee. The change was not to the benefit of the enemy. The nomad pulled a pair of daggers from his belt and fought like a dervish.

Down the path, the Coltsfoot twins leapt from their steeds and battled back to back. The brothers moved in perfect harmony, anticipating each other's moves and thrusts. They fought as if they were of a single mind and extensions of the same body.

Dool swung a heavy axe over his head and cleaved through the enemy from his steed's back. The horse bucked and kicked, a furious force in its own right. The creature must have been as bloodthirsty as the man mounted upon its saddle, for it fought with a stubborn tenacity that planted its powerful hooves against each enemy's weak points to shatter bone and dislocate joints.

Sian pressed his back to a tree for cover and faced two enemies of his own. His sword appeared small in comparison to the large blades wielded against him.

Metal clashed and sparks flew as the young warrior fought desperately for his life. His grandfather had been right all along. He wasn't ready, but he would have to quickly ready himself if he wanted to return to his wife!

"Sian!" From horseback, Junua raised her stave toward the sky and summoned a bolt of lightning. It crashed into one of the approaching men. It blinded the surviving attacker, and Sian swiftly separated the disoriented man's head from his shoulders.

"Thanks!" he called back to her.

Beneath the assault of swords and magic, the enemy ranks became blessedly thin. They grinned at each other and approached their horses, speaking of their good fortune. So far, many days into their travel, the road to Darknoor had been easier than anticipated. Along the way, they had roused the attention of many other villages, informing them of the danger Matta Dora posed to all of them. If left unchecked, her evil would only grow and continue to swell until it overtook all of Sinead.

Village leaders pledged their aid, promised to prepare their men and follow in their stead. They needed only to help pave the way.

"We will win this," Furil said, wiping the blood from his blade before he sheathed it again.

"Matta Dora has no hope against us. Her soldiers are weak and ill-trained," Dool said as he mounted his horse.

"You speak too soon. These are only mortal men of flesh and blood. These are neither Doom Fliers nor the golems under her command. Greater dangers await us," Junua said quietly from horseback.

"It is too early to speak of victory. As the woman says, we must persevere whether the road appears easy or not."

"Ch! We will defeat her and restore peace to Sinead before the other armies ever arrive," Giber boasted. His twin grinned at him.

They spoke too soon, for their good fortune was short-lived and nearly became a massacre. As he stood beside his brother, Serlig stumbled and fell after a razor-edged arrow pierced his heart from the thick of the trees. His twin screamed and dashed forward toward the unseen assailant. He cleaved the soldier who struck his brother into two, but justice could not restore Serlig to life.

But it was too late. Next, Furil fell beneath a surprise attack from above and was left for dead on the frosted ground. Another dark soldier leapt from amidst the overhanging branches of the tree and rushed at Sian. He moved as fast as a demon from the depths of the unknown, twisting and whirling beneath the storm of attacks from the Reindeer Keep survivors. Even Junua's lightning bolt sailed over his head and struck a tree. The scent of burning wood filled their nostrils and smoke rose toward the sky.

"He is one of her assassins! Quickly! We must take him down now before we're all doomed!" Yorteze cried. His wooden projectiles hit the cold ground, missing their mark multiple times. Sian was pressed backwards, forced to rapidly block one strike after another.

It ended when a lucky blow from Giber sank into the assassin's back. When it was over, the raucous sounds of battle gave way to abrupt silence, only to be filled with *grieving wails. They had lost two in the blink of an eye and there was nothing to bring them back.*

Before her eyes, the illusion within the scrying water faded into the dismal black of night. It seemed much darker to Immandra now, reflecting her own inner despair. "Is that all?" she whispered in a tiny voice.

"That is all we know, dear one. What the rain brings and the waterbird sings... We know nothing more."

"Perhaps I should go to the fairy queen?" Immandra questioned. She grasped at straws, eager to uncover any useful news. Would Sibba receive her on such short notice?

"An excellent idea. If she cannot help you, no one can."

Immandra quickly brushed the snow from her skirt and walked away from the lake with her warm shawl tightly wrapped around her shoulders. The wind seemed colder now than it ever had before.

***

Lady Sibba, Queen of the Fairies, lived in the forest as all other matriarchs before her. A hollowed tree, petrified to glorious, golden perfection, guarded her privacy while rumors claimed she dwelled deep below the surface of the earth in a magical wonderland.

A fairy maiden greeted Immandra at the door and quickly ushered her in from the cold. Her glacial blue eyes seemed friendly in the glowing crystals lining the receiving chamber. A warm, inviting sense of comfort immediately surrounded the weary traveler, permeating every inch of her tired body. She had woken at dawn after a fitful sleep, and then walked for hours through the depths of the forest against the bitter winds.

Immandra's teeth chattered uncontrollably. "It's S-s-s-Sian. I m-m-must see the queen," she managed to finally utter between her involuntary shivers. The frigid conditions outside had reduced her to a near popsicle.

"Of course. Your arrival was expected, young one. Please, follow me. Lady Sibba awaits you."

She expected me? Immandra thought. Her heart filled with relief, driving her hastened steps. She quickly followed the young fairy woman down the spiraling staircase into a brightly lit, crystalline chamber far beneath the ground. The entire cavern shined in rainbows hues, holding every comfort a queen could ever need.

Beautiful, radiant, and benevolent as ever, Sibba rose from her seat upon a glimmering dais and crossed the room to approach Immandra. "What may I do for you, child?" the fairy queen asked. Without hesitation, she heated Immandra's hands between her own, seeming more generous with each passing moment. The chattering of her teeth promptly ceased as unnatural heat and fairy magic infused her body.

It's all worth it for Sian, Immandra thought. *I need to know his fate. I must know that he's alive.* "Sian and the others have not returned."

Sibba's charming smile began to fade. "This is as I feared. I foresaw your arrival and knew you would come on this unforgiving winter day. I believe I may have what you seek." She spun on a heel and moved with graceful steps to lead Immandra deeper within the safety of her home. Sibba's black hair fell over her shoulder in an intricate plait, frozen dewdrops sparkling like diamonds against the dark strands. Pale blue silk hugged her slim form, representing the current season. The last time Immandra had seen her, on the night of her wedding, the Queen's gown had shimmered in shades of lavender and tender green. It was no less beautiful now, but she couldn't truly admire it while her husband's fate remained unknown to her.

"I will search for him, but I warn you, young one. What you seek may not be what you wish to see."

"Please," she beseeched the queen with tears glimmering in her indigo eyes.

The two women leaned over a glowing sphere. It first reflected the battle revealed by the waters, failing to yield any new knowledge to Immandra.

"I've seen this part," Immandra said in despair. "I need to know what happened next. Did they all survive the next encounter? Did the attackers come back?"

"Patience, young one. Let us look deeper." Sibba waved her hands over the crystal, her fingers glowing in the same pulsing hues of color. The battle faded into nothingness and a new scene shimmered into being.

Giber wept over a cairn of rock and Yorteze spoke ancient sylvan prayers over two mounds. The image shifted again, speeding forward, giving the impression of many hours passing. Days perhaps. In the deep woods, the light was always dark. Day and night seemed the same. When it finally solidified into a clear view, Darknoor Castle loomed in the distance. Wide plain, dotted with stone statues, spread between its imposing walls and the forest edge. Approaching from the thicket, the remaining four warriors rode toward the empty stretch of desolate plain. Above them, dark shapes appeared in the sky.

"What in the hell are those?" Dool lifted his hand to shade his eyes. The rest of the group did the same, straining to see.

"I can't see," Sian muttered, squinting against the sun. Its light seemed blinding after their weeks in the forest.

The elongated, serpentine neck of the scaled creature, led from a lithely-muscled frame, kept aloft by a pair of powerful wings. The membranous, leathery appendages spanned for several yards and were, in fact, strong enough to bear the weight of an adult man in full armor. Each terrifying creature possessed four monstrous feet tipped in curved, black talons.

"Doom Fliers..." Giber whispered.

"Draw your weapons!" Dool shouted.

The Doom Fliers swiftly advanced with a rapid descent, outnumbering the heroes down below. Each of the terrifying beasts landed and threw open its beak in a threatening display. This revealed a multitude of intimidating, yellowing teeth and a serrated tongue.

Sian first fell back and raised his sword in a defensive gesture, but the weapon appeared no more harmful than a toothpick, compared to his mighty foe. Yorteze stood beside him and shot one of his living bolts at the nearest beast. It reared back and flared its wings, shrieking in defiance.

"I will do what I can to keep the others from reaching us!" Junua cried. She slipped her staff between her leg and the body of her mount, then clapped both of her hands together as if in prayer. The volume of her chant rose louder and louder until a shimmering wall of arcane power exploded around them. Had she released her spell a second faster, they would have had a single foe to face.

A second Doom Flier had snuck beneath the veil of magic just in time.

"Aim for the neck or switch to bows! Your weapons will glance off of their hides," Yorteze cried in warning.

Proving the sylvan correct, Dool's axe became worthless in the heat of the battle. The creatures moved with the lightning-quick reflexes of snakes, and when a blow did land against one, his weapon merely bounced away. They darted out with their beaks to fend him off, capitalizing on the shorter reach of his weapon, but never allowing him the killing stroke he desired.

Each scream and piercing wail struck fear into Sian's heart. His eyes widened with terror until he desperately stumbled back on the defensive. Giber slashed like a madman, but his sword was useless against the scaled hides. Sharp claws grabbed the man by his shoulders and he was lifted into the air.

"Make for the statues!" Dool cried. "They're some cover at least!"

"No, you fool!" Junua cried. "My magic is the only thing protecting us!"

Dool made it five steps beyond the arcane shield. A circling Doom Flier screeched, and red beams shot from its eyes at the warrior's retreating back. He froze, his limbs locking mid-step, and he became stone like the statues he had hoped to seek shelter behind.

"We can't hold off much longer!" Sian yelled above the chaotic clang of swords against the armored beasts.

"I will fight to the last!" Yorteze answered him in a defiant cry.

"I won't give up!" Junua agreed.

"Me too," replied Sian.

The two women leaned over the shimmering image. Immandra bent over so far her nose nearly touched the green sphere, her indigo eyes wide. No matter how she stared or angled her eyes to gaze into its mystical surface, it remained a simple, opaque globe. She gave in to her frustration and shook it wildly between her hands until the vibrant emerald glow dispersed into a thousand shimmering motes of color. They reformed gradually but no images of Sian were born from the coalescing beads of light. "What happened? I need to see the rest. This doesn't tell me what's happened to Sian," Immandra cried in distress.

Sibba never lost her kind smile, but she did take the seer's tool away from her with a light and firm touch. "Gently, my child. This is a very delicate instrument."

"But Lady Sibba, I must know... I... I must know what's happened to Sian. Maybe he's injured." The very thought brought immense pain to her heart. She pictured Sian lying wounded upon some desolate plain, defending his life from Doom Fliers and other fiends.

"This was only a glimpse of what is to come, young one." Sibba's graceful hand passed over the sphere, swirling the cloudy substance inside without forming a picture. "Wherever he is, my magic cannot reach him now." She set the globe upon the pedestal where it belonged and slid her arms around Immandra's shoulders. The fairy queen embraced her until her shoulders ceased shaking and the sobs subsided.

"What should I do, Lady Sibba?"

Sibba released her and stepped back, her thoughtful gaze traveling toward a small stonework vase upon a marble pillar. "Perhaps the genie can aid you. He is an unpleasant old fellow, but he has powers unlike mine."

"I'd have to go to the Forbidden Mountain…"

"It's not really as bad as people think," Sibba assured her in a gentle voice.

"But he is a mean man. An awful man. Everyone says he brings doom and sorrow in his wake."

Sibba trailed her hand tenderly over Immandra's hair. "Things are not always as they seem, and this goes for people as well. Remember this, Immandra. You should never judge one only by their outward appearance."

Immandra nodded, but the tension in her gut remained. "If you truly think he can help."

"You will never know unless you try. But his home is far and you will never arrive before the night. Stay here, warm yourself, and with the rising of the sun, I will send you on your way."

***

"Milady, will you not tell her?"

Sibba turned and cast a sorrowful smile upon the fairy woman who slipped into her room after Immandra stepped out for the evening. Her handmaiden crossed over and took Sibba's hands into her own.

"The girl holds enough worry in her heart, Kirial. I cannot add to it."

Kirial drew Sibba to take a seat on a pile of silken pillows. Sibba closed her eyes while the other woman unwound her heavy plaits and loosened the many adornments from her hair.

"But she is so young. Untested. And Matta--"

"I know," Sibba said, bowing her head. "But in this I cannot do more than I have. I cannot be the one to put a weapon into Immandra's hands, whether it be knowledge or a sword. Not against my own children, Kirial." Sorrow weighed the Queen's voice.

"It has been many years since the twins left us and even longer since their father passed."

"I often wonder if things would have been different had they known him." Sibba held out her hand and a sparkling swirl of wind formed above her open palm. The colors and sparks coalesced into an image of a man. Bright green eyes shined from a face framed with pale blonde hair. A darker golden scruff spread across his chin and jaw.

"A handsome man," Kirial commented. Her periwinkle eyes crinkled at the corners with her smile. "Of course, he must have been, to capture the heart of a fairy like you, milady."

"Handsome, kind, brave, strong... Kellan was all of those things and more. But there was also darkness in him. Ambition."

"You have never spoken to me of how he died."

Sibba closed her hand and the image broke apart into glistening motes. "He sought to sail the distant seas. Often, he would return with treasures and lay them at my feet, but I wanted none of them. Only his heart. Still he returned to the seas. The children grew, but he had no eyes for them. Again I turned away his gifts and asked him to stay. But the crystalline halls of my home were not enough. He wanted more. He left to raid the waters. This time he did not return. His ship was lost in the great storms surrounding the Lost Isles. Many times, I warned him to end his search."

Kirial set the brush aside. "And so bitterness grew in the twins' hearts?"

"And so…" Sibba replied softly. "And my own. I should have become a better mother, but I allowed mourning to cloud my judgment. It consumed my days and nights. I can't help but feel in part that some of this is my doing and my responsibility. Had I done more for them…"

"Will you not do more for her? Give her some tools, Milady? The girl cannot go and face them unarmed and without a weapon."

"No, I have given her all I can. This is a path Immandra must tread by her own choosing. I cannot instruct her to send them to their deaths. Not when I've wronged them so as a mother and sown this hatred in their hearts."

"Then let us help her in another way, Milady. Child of our people, or not, she will not long survive the cold."

Sibba smiled back over her shoulder. "Yes. Please see it is done."

Chapter Six

INFATUATION

Of the five remaining adventurers approaching Darknoor, a single handsome face gained Matta Dora's interest. In observing their progress, she had learned only a single thing about the youthful warrior.

His name was Sian.

She watched him and she waited, plotting devious intentions all the while as the hunting party made their way toward her castle. Much like a spider tending her web, she knew that he would play into her hands easily enough. "I want one brought to me. I care not what you do with the others," she commented, giving a flippant wave of her hand. "Perhaps you should keep the Sorceress who dares to trespass against my lands."

"Ah, you know I love them spirited, sister." Mizar practically licked his lips. The terrified women in the village didn't dare deny them, for they knew what would happen to their lovers and sons if Matta discovered their unpleasant attitudes.

"Which one do you fancy, my dear sister?"

Matta Dora and Mizar stood over a wide, shallow dish of blood and watched the battle through the eyes of their pets. The carcass of the princess' serving boy lay discarded in the corner. Like many who served Matta Dora, he had done nothing to earn his fate, and yet he had paid the ultimate price for merely being in the wrong place at the wrong time.

The woman pointed a silver painted nail at the image of Sian.

"I want that one alive," she repeated herself. She practically purred her desires out loud, eyes focused upon Sian's rugged features.

"A mere boy," Mizar said with a scoff. "Don't you ever tire of playing with children? I would have expected your attentions to fall to the warrior beside him, or perhaps to the exotic sylvan."

"Not when they entice me as much as this one. I wish to tame him as my own and to break his spirit. The young ones are the most defiant, are they not?" A lusty smile raised the corners of her mouth. "He *will* be mine." She glanced back to the slain corpse, expression bored. "Besides, I am without a champion worthy of serving my every need. What a fine trophy he shall make. I deserve him!" She slammed her fist upon the table, suddenly stirred into a great anger.

Mizar's unreadable features remained unchanging through the beginnings of her tantrum. He watched for a time until, at long last, he leaned down and kissed the pointed tip of her nose. "As you wish, my dear Matta. The boy shall remain untouched. The rest will know their demise shortly."

"Good. They can die upon their swords or join their pitiful country folk in our dungeons. You have been enjoying the gifts, I hope?"

Mizar chuckled again and gently took the bowl from Matta Dora's hands. He set it aside on the table then drew his sister in close. "A whole new herd to groom as you see fit, sweet Matta. The children clean your halls as we speak and their mothers dare not defy my wishes. I even found you a new baker."

Matta sniffed in disdain. "Walk with me then."

They strolled arm in arm through the bleak castle hallways. The two siblings made a striking pair, both tall and lean, with pale hair and sharply angled features. Mizar wore his hair short, never any longer than his shoulders. Matta preferred hers long. The silver-bright curls fell past her hips.

"With each passing day, Matta, your power grows and spreads. The snows have spread far past the Forbidden Mountain. Mother wouldn't dare to make a move against--"

"Don't call that wilting flower a mother," Matta interrupted him sharply. "It surprises me none that she has no spine to face us." She scoffed, expressing her disdain for the woman who birthed them. The twins viewed Sibba as a vessel and little more, the inattentive meat who brought them into this world, but failed to see their potential. "Soft, as always. My, I wonder what she plans to do... Will she withdraw deeper into the forests, or shall she hold out against our invasion."

"She will withdraw," Mizar predicted. "She would never allow us the pleasure of trampling over her cold corpse."

"I want to see her dead. I want to see her begging and pleading for her life before I deliver death to her. Why can't we strike against the Emerald Forest now, Mizar? Why allow her to escape with her life?" The cold Princess of Darkness glowered ahead, radiating cold anger from every pore. Mizar calmed her with a soothing south to her hair.

"Dear sister, what she chooses to do should mean nothing to you. The point is, Matta, soon we will hold sway over all of Sinead."

"Fine. Send out our Doom Fliers and fetch me my present." Matta ordered. "Now."

***

"Your shield can't hold forever! We should retreat!" Sian cried above the clash of clanging swords.

"I thought you said you would fight to the last?" Junua called back. Her strained smile wavered and entirely dissipated as she nearly sagged in the saddle beneath the force of her own immense concentration.

"I would, but this is suicide! They spied us from the very moment we arrived to Darknoor. We never had a chance," Giber said. He grunted and swung his sword into the thick neck of the Doom Flier. Sian faced it from the other side, flanking it with Giber. Blood stained his armor, glistened on his blade, and the foul taste of it invaded his mouth.

Sian struck the lucky blow that penetrated the beaten hide. His blade sank to the hilt between the neck and shoulder. As it defiantly screamed, Giber gave a roar of his own and brought his brother's axe into the Doom

Flier's neck. The head flopped free and rolled away.

Sweat stung Junua's eyes. It was too early to cheer while more of the monsters soared toward their protective magical shell. "Are you okay, Yorteze?"

"I will live." Yorteze took in a few ragged, exhausted breaths. His blood resembled tree sap, running thick and sticky down his skin where it congealed into a golden amber color. He'd stopped to wrap several linen bandages around his arms and injured torso.

"What do you suggest we do?" Giber asked. "I won't leave. I swore on my brother's grave that I would fight to avenge him."

"Can you do that if you're dead? Think, Giber! We came to fight, but we must not throw our lives away," Sian argued.

"The child has a point," Junua said. "I cannot maintain this shield forever. It is true. We must make our decision now. The other villages must be warned and told to move with haste. We have seen the results of the army that approaches, the aftermath of their march. They will cut a swathe straight to North Sky Village and carry on to Reindeer Keep if we allow them to continue."

"Ride," Yorteze said quietly. The sylvan's head turned toward the approaching army. "We will hold them for as long as we may. If I should die, let it not be in vain."

"Agreed!" Giber said.

Sian gazed at the marching wall of aggressors, each bloodthirsty warrior more eager to engage them than the last. He shuddered. "I won't leave you," he spoke bravely.

"If I leave, you'll be unshielded," Junua warned

them. "Are you sure of that?"

"Ride, woman!" Giber shouted. He slapped her horse on the flank, with the flat of his blade, startling the mare. She bolted forward as Junua's spell fizzled.

"Don't any of you dare die!" she called. The shield shimmered, shattering into thousands of glimmering specks. She didn't gaze behind her to watch their battle. She couldn't.

She had to ride as if her very life and the fate of the world depended on her. The wind whipped through her hair and scraggly tree branches scraped her face, reaching like decrepit fingers from the beyond. She urged her horse into a full gallop. They flew and the world became a dismal blur of colors around her. Doom Fliers gave chase from above, seeking to restrain her for the enemy.

"I won't let you win!" she cried as the first laser of petrification beamed toward her. She ducked forward and hugged against the neck of her mount. The beam narrowly missed its target. "Ha!"

In the dead forest bordering Darknoor, no leaves grew upon the frost-covered branches. Barren twigs were too thick, too sharp, and not quite brittle enough for the Doom Fliers to descend and face her in melee combat. It was all the better for her. Junua raised her staff with one hand and gave an arcane shout. With her words of power, magic took form in the skies above. Her power coalesced into a fierce windstorm, churning the blackened clouds.

I can't let them catch me.

One of the men cried out behind her, the voice lacking the depth and timbre associated with Giber. *Not*

Sian! She thought in dismay. The boy should have never accompanied the group. He was too young and too inexperienced. Yet there was nothing better than to die a warrior's death and the glory of battle carried no age requirement.

"Faster!" she cried to her horse.

The copper-hued mare put on a valiant burst of speed, responding to her call. Her hooves tossed up clods of dirt and leaf matter. Hot breaths steamed from her nostrils.

Lightning sizzled from the sky and struck the wing of one of the Doom Fliers. The creature shrieked and began a hasty descent, spiraling out of control. The mutated bird crashed into the heavy thicket of trees and diseased bushes to Junua's left. Another took its place in the pursuit. With a feral shriek, it descended, bursting through the wintered landscape without concern for damaging its own body. Junua rushed through a chant of arcane words and twisted the wind through the trees. The force knocked her pursuer off course. Blown toward the heavier branches, the flier was impaled upon a broken limb.

They were nearly in the clear.

Arrows coasted toward her, fired from the bows of hidden marksmen lurking in the trees. One came dangerously close to striking her mare in its hindquarters, but it skimmed through her flowing tail instead. The rest entirely missed and were unable to pin the fleet-footed creature. The second volley harmlessly pinged against an erected magical shield, too tough for their mundane arrows to penetrate.

They had us surrounded this whole time, she

realized. *They wanted us to make it as far as we did.*

The last Doom Flier waited and struck when Junua broke through and into a clearing. Her steed reared back, but the sorceress kept her seat.

"Your warped pets will not detain me, Matta Dora." Junua stared the creature down and spoke to the eyes behind its dark vision. "Your abuses of magic will not go unpunished."

The landed creature spread its wings and screeched at her in defiance. It snapped its beak towards her mount, but Junua smacked it aside with her staff. The resounding crack echoed across the small, snowy glade.

She spun the weapon over her head and called upon her next spell. Junua drew the cold beneath them and formed it into deadly spikes of hard-packed snow. At her word, the projectiles flew at the flier and slammed against its hide and wings. Membrane ripped beneath the assault and the creature screamed in fury and pain.

I don't have any choice. I'll have to ford the river, she thought. Frost glistened over the surface of the river ahead. Its depth was unknown, untested, and was a possible death for her and the horse. She called down another bolt of skyfire and directed it toward the river. It obliterated the icy shell and steamed thickly.

"Go!" she urged the horse. They raced into the water, taking their chances. They proved the river to be little more than a stream, for they had swam it and emerged from the other side within moments.

Escaping Darknoor was easier said than done, but as Junua crossed its perimeter borders, she couldn't help but glance back over her shoulders and fear for the men she'd left behind.

Chapter Seven

A DEAL WITH A WITCH

As promised, Immandra left at dawn, and this time she left with higher spirits. A night spent among the faeries had filled her soul with lightness and hope. Their quiet cheer warmed her from within, far better than the rich stews and sweet teas they had served her.

The queen saw her outfitted with clothes meant for cold travel. Soft leathers kept her warm, sturdy boots protected her feet, and a furred cloak kept out the chill winds. Lastly, Lady Sibba had kissed her brow and told her two words- keep hope.

Immandra clung to the advice and held it close in her heart.

Sibba claimed the journey to the Forbidden Mountain wasn't bad, but it was every bit as harrowing a journey as the stories claimed. Immandra traveled a serpentine path over a steep and treacherous incline, nearly losing her footing once or twice along the way. The snow-crusted mountain became a deathly hazard during the winter's season, but she had become absolutely determined to discover Sian's fate. She couldn't turn back in good conscience and would have scrambled up the mountain slope on all fours if necessary. Once or twice, the snowfall began anew, forcing Immandra to seek refuge behind an outcropping of rock.

She found the genie's home at the very top.

Walls of polished stone rose up from the rocky ground and graceful pillars lined the cobbled path that led up to the carved wooden door. It hardly looked as she expected for the cantankerous hermit. With her heart pounding and her breaths heaving, she knocked on the door and silently prayed her trip was not in vain.

"Go away! I'm busy!" a sharp voice called out from inside.

"Kaitan Speedwell, I must speak with you." She huddled against the cold winds with her arms folded against her chest for warmth. Rubbing them was the most she could do for a tiny ounce of comfort. Up here, high in the peaks, the cloak hardly kept out the winds.

She heard footsteps followed by the sound of multiple locks turning. The door cracked up, barely allowing her a glance inside.

"Oh, it's you." Kaitan's disinterested voice shattered her spirits. "What do you want, girl?"

Immandra clasped her hands before her. "P-p-please, I need your help. You are m-m-my only hope." Her teeth painfully chattered in her mouth. How did trackers and hunters ever accomplish anything in such horrible weather?

"Me? Help? That's highly irregular. People never

come to me for help." He didn't budge from the threshold of the door, but Immandra didn't move either. She couldn't face Sian's mother if she returned without any good news. "Come in," he consented after a moment of silence, maybe even in disbelief.

As she crossed into the mountain home, she experienced a quiet sense of pity for the man who seemingly lived alone in a quiet dwelling of stone and chiseled rock. The polished exterior held beauty of its own, but inside, it seemed as empty as the man who lurked within its walls. There were no friends, no family, no one at all.

"Sit down then. I told you on your wedding night, didn't I? Grief, separation, bad luck were to happen. I told all of it to you, but you didn't want to believe a word I told you." He seemed satisfied, but Immandra couldn't determine whether his contentment was a product of her unhappiness or his accurate prophecy. Maybe it was from both.

A tear tracked down her cheek and promptly ended his crowing and gloats. "I'm sorry," he said quietly. "Go on then and warm yourself beside the fire, girl. You're shaking snow all over my floor." Unlike Sibba, he didn't enfold her into a magical embrace or even set his hand on her shoulder. He silenced and set a steaming mug onto the low table before her seat, and then he sat opposite from her. His bragging ended. It was replaced by a strange display of empathy that granted Immandra all the time she needed to cry out her tense emotions while warming her hands on the cup.

"Thank you," Immandra whispered quietly. "I didn't mean to bother you, but we cannot go another day without discovering what has happened to him and the other adventurers. Their families are all worried and none of us know what to do. The waters sent me to Lady Sibba, but then she sent me to you."

"I see. Then perhaps you are not as selfish as I previously thought, girl. Let's see what we can do. We'll begin with the bones, and if that doesn't work, I have some other tricks up my sleeve. The runes can be used too, if necessary," he humbly offered with a dip of his head. He shook the leather sack of polished bone runes, and offered her a reassuring smile.

"Selfish?" She swiped at her damp, blotched cheeks.

"You speak of more than just your husband."

"Of course I do. I worry for Sian, yes, but I care for all of them. They have all gone to protect *us*. How could I not care for the fate of them all?"

Kaitan held up a hand, palm out, and gestured her to silence. "And so I will grant your request. I will see what I can see."

As the last of the daylight hours dwindled and the sun slowly sank below the horizon, Immandra felt her own hopes diminishing more and more with each failed trick. Kaitan's enthusiasm waned until he sat hunched over his tools of divination, wearing a forlorn expression to match her own disappointed features. Nothing had worked. Not a single one.

"I can't believe it. I couldn't see a single thing, and this has never happened to me before. Not once," he told her in a quiet, broken tone. "Please don't tell anyone."

"My word," Immandra promised.

"Oh, thank you. Thank you," Kaitan said in relief. He leapt up from his seat and paced across the room.

"Now let us see... Aha! Yes! Zyda Bitternel, in the Enchanted Forest. She is old and irritable, and her powers are great. She is also much closer to the source of your dilemma and the place you wish to scry, but... she is expensive. Such power as hers does not come without immense cost, you see. I fear for what she may ask of you, the price may be far much than you are willing to pay."

Immandra's heart sank. "They say the Enchanted Forest is a creepy place, but if that is where I will find help then there is where I will go."

"It used to be beautiful once, you know. Filled with laughing pixies and playful tree spirits. Faeries danced there in the moonlight. But that was long ago." He looked sad as he relayed the story.

"What happened?"

"Oh, the usual." Kaitan shrugged and shook off his melancholy. "Dark magics tainted it over the years. Sucked away the happiness."

"Matta Dora...?" Immandra ventured uncertainly. She had the uneasy feeling that her guess was incorrect.

"Zyda," Kaitan replied bluntly. He looked Immandra in the eye. "I mean it when I said she is expensive and her price may be one you cannot afford. She does nothing out of kindness, so do not believe you can sway her heart. She has none."

Immandra rose to her feet, filled with renewed trepidation and fear for her beloved. With every hour that she sought to discover his outcome, his chances of survival slimmed. "Thank you, Kaitan. Truly. I will find my way to Zyda and do what I must."

"A blizzard comes, and the sun has set," the man

grumbled. "Take your rest here, gather your strength. Death will find you on this mountain if you try and go at night."

"I couldn't--" Her empty stomach rumbled and gurgled with hunger. Her meal with the fairies seemed days ago and her small noontime meal had hardly sated her appetite. The mountain climb had sapped her of strength.

"Your belly says you could," Kaitan quipped as he left his seat. He returned with a crust of bread, a stone bowl of soup fragrant with spices, and a mug of fresh water. She voraciously tore into the meal with the appetite of a starving warlord. Kaitan chuckled when she dragged her finger over the interior of the bowl to remove the last of the creamy residue.

She settled beneath a blanket near the hearth, where she didn't budge until morning when she awakened to the sizzling smell of fresh eggs in goat butter. She ate ravenously again, drank several mugs of steaming tea, and braced herself for the walk down.

To Immandra's surprise, a massive antlered riding stag awaited her beyond the heavy stone door of Kaitan's temple.

"Meet Hessop. He's agreed to bear you to the Enchanted Forest. The trip will take a few days instead of weeks now."

Hessop wore no saddle, only a massive pile of comfortable blankets upon his silky white back. His fur fell in a shaggy pattern down his heavily muscled sides, but Immandra suspected it would have been cushion enough, even without the riding blankets. For a halter, twin braids of leather circled the creature's jowls and looped behind his head to connect behind the antlers.

These were loose and easily held in her hand. It was more for her own security than to guide the intelligent creature in any way.

Immandra didn't know what came over her. She whirled on the spot and threw her arms around the creaky old stubborn man and hugged him tightly. Even more surprising, just as she feared she had insulted or offended him with her show of gratitude, he embraced her in return.

"It is my pleasure to accompany you on this journey, Immandra Stillwater. I will be your faithful companion to the end," Hessop greeted her.

Immandra dipped down into a polite curtsy and returned Hessop's greeting. Her fingers then touched his silken mane and smoothed through the lustrous ivory strands. Hessop was beautiful to her eyes, and she would have to be blind not to find him an amazing creature. Her heart swelled with joy. "Thank you for agreeing to aid us, Hessop. I appreciate this greatly," she told him. Her head then turned to Kaitan and she smiled at him as well. "And thank you again. Thank you, Kaitan."

"I have but one last thing to give to you, Immandra. Take this. You will know best when it is time for it to see use." He handed her a slim dagger within a leather sheath. Beautiful, ornately carved ivory vines and leaves traveled over the hilt of the blade. It was longer than most knives, practically a short sword but elegant and light in her hold.

"I do not know how to use such a weapon," she told him doubtfully.

"It will come to you when the time is right. One should never go on an adventure unprepared. It is dangerous to travel these roads without a weapon. Surely you did not intend to go empty-handed?"

Immandra sighed. "To be honest, we didn't take it into consideration. I was so desperate to know what happened to Sian. I didn't plan any kind of adventure. I'm not packed for distant traveling and I... I never spoke of such to the others in Reindeer Keep Village." She felt foolish now as she thought about how hastily she had flown from the village in pursuit of the truth. Now she intended to go on a grand rescue and she knew nothing at all about how to protect herself along the way.

"Then it is all the better that the fairy queen sent you to me. Be well and be brave, my dear. Good luck. You will need it on this journey. I will send word to the Stillwaters to notify them of your travel."

Hessop needed no direction. The wise mount picked his way surefootedly down the steep mountain with practiced ease as if he had done it a thousand times. If Immandra were on foot, she wouldn't have made it to stable ground until nightfall.

Kuiper Appleroot awaited her at the bottom. He quickly began to bounce up and down on his booted feet upon recognizing her on the majestic beast. "There you are! I feared for you! I worried! I fretted and looked for you!" he cried. "Why did you come without me?"

"Lady Sibba sent me to speak to Kaitan. How did you find me?"

"The mountain birds saw your climb, and Roxy smelled your scent just beneath the newly fallen snow." The white, snowy fox beside him gazed at Immandra with disapproval.

"I'm sorry," Immandra apologized. She held tightly

to Hessop's halter and satin mane with one hand for balance as she leaned down to retrieve her friends. Roxy scampered over her arm, but Kuiper grasped her fingers and was easily drawn upon Hessop's back. With Kuiper seated in front of her and Roxy riding on her shoulder, they set off for the road leading to the Enchanted Forest.

"Are you sure this is a good idea?" Kuiper cast a fearful glance at the thick wall of gnarled trees.

Roxy peeked her head out from beneath Immandra's hair and sniffed the air. "This place makes me uneasy," the little fox said, her ears laid back flat against her head.

"I feel the same, but what else can I do? I must learn of Sian's fate. You two have no need to continue further with me. I didn't even intend to return to the village, to be honest," Immandra confessed. She quickly suppressed her shame, reminded of the task ahead of her. For Sian and the other heroes of Reindeer Keep Village, she would have to be strong and determined. She couldn't ever doubt herself or the path ahead of her. Furthermore, she had to find out if the rest of the villages had rallied together their own warriors.

Kuiper huffed indignantly. "I would never allow you to go in there by yourself. Who do you think I am? *I'm* your friend and I will use my skills and wisdom to protect you."

"Ha!" Roxy snorted. "And what skills are those? Fishing? Pah! All you do is sit by the lake in silence. As for wisdom, a fallen log has more than you."

"Will you stop that? I don't need you two quarreling along the way." Immandra shook her head and continued to guide Hessop down to the forest edge.

"Who's fighting? We were just trying to kill some

time, is all. Wait, I see the path leading deeper into the forest," Kuiper said.

A narrow track led into the trees, barely wide enough to be called a proper path. It was more than they had discovered so far.

"Yes, I believe you're right," Immandra agreed quietly. Hessop balked at first then the graceful creature turned onto the track, using his antlers to brush aside the dried branches barring the way.

All around them, the trees appeared cracked and dry. They also seemed dead. No leaves grew from the splintered branches, which rustled in the cold breeze. The wind reminded Immandra of whispers and cackling laughter, following them, but also increasing in volume and frequency the deeper they travelled. To her great fortune, the creepy atmosphere of the forest silenced Roxy and Kuiper, ending their argument and allowing her to travel in relative peace with only the weight of her worries on her mind. The trio rode in silence, each casting fretting glances around and behind them.

Immandra felt as though eyes followed her. Her skin prickled, sweat beaded at her brow, but she never caught sight of anyone or anything beyond the trees.

It turned out that Hessop was a creature of few words. He had readily spoken to her outside of the genie's temple, but he had little to offer while in the company of Kuiper and Roxy. Immandra wondered if he disliked the bickering between her friends as much as she did. Sometimes, it certainly made her want to remain quiet as well.

They made camp before nightfall. Gloomy darkness settled over the forest and made their fire seem pitiful. It was a small speck of ember and orange in the deep black surroundings. They huddled around its meager warmth.

"I hope we can do what we have to do and get out of here quickly. I'm not so fond of this place," Kuiper whispered.

"Why are you whispering?" Immandra asked in the same low tone. His little bald scalp felt chilly beneath her hand. She fashioned him a head-covering from a bit of her own scarf and he gratefully smiled at her.

"I have a feeling that more than the forest is listening," he replied.

"So?!" demanded Roxy. Despite her teacup sized body, Roxy's voice was loud and boisterous. It rang over the trees and scattered the birds huddled amidst the barren branches. "Do we have anything to hide? As for me, *I'm* not the least afraid."

A shrill howl rang through the air, freezing Immandra's blood. Roxy quickly leapt into the larger human's pocket where she sought refuge, quivering fearfully. She stuck out only her face, with ears and a pink nose visible with two large eyes. "

"Your bravery is admirable," Kuiper commented. "*I'll* be telling stories about it to your children and grandchildren. They'll all be very proud."

"You wouldn't dare," Roxy hissed.

"Oh yeah? Try me."

"Cut it out," Immandra interrupted.

"I concur," Hessop rumbled in his deep voice. Their riding stag seemed to have a longer fuse than Immandra when it came to their arguments. He had remained silent for a time, but that quickly faded. "There greater things at stake than your need to belittle one another."

"Thank you, Hessop," Immandra told him gratefully. "We'll need to get some rest before the morning. Tomorrow will be a tough day," she told them. Hessop settled at one side, his large body providing a windbreak. He seemed immune to the cold, thanks to his heavy covering of white fur. He was the warmest thing she had ever felt.

Immandra nestled close against their new friend's powerful torso while Kuiper and Roxy snuggled in near, flanking her from each side. With the stag's blankets drawn atop them, the small group finally found rest.

***

The thinning branches of the dying forest revealed a dilapidated hut. The shoddy door hung on aging, rusted hinges, and through its opening, Immandra saw an old woman hunched above a stovetop. Her bent spine curved like a sage's staff, and her nose competed with the beak of the mightiest waterfowl.

The steam wafting from the pot stank, lacking the clean and spicy perfume of the tea Kaitan brewed in his mountaintop home. This smelled murky, like fetid swamp water.

Kuiper shrank back when the old hag turned her malicious face toward them. "Oh my. Perhaps I can… wait for you somewhere. I don't feel very sociable right now," he whispered.

"Coward!" Roxy cried. "Afraid of an old lady! All of gnome-kind will shake with laughter for days when I tell them."

"Just remember last night. I have things to tell too."

"Be quiet," Immandra chastened them. She dismounted the white stag and picked her way into the clearing. Kuiper clung to the glossy, silken mane of Hessop, but Roxy uttered another sly taunt and insult to his gnomish pride. He toppled off into the dirt with a pitiful *oof* and scrambled after Immandra's tracks in the snow. Apparently, he'd decided the company of the old crone was preferable to Roxy's acerbic personality.

"Venerable Zyda Bitternel, I bid you greetings. Kaitan Speedwell sent me to seek your wisdom. I am Immandra Stillwater, formerly from the Linden clan."

"Can't you see I'm busy?" The crone's voice crackled like splitting wood. Her harsh eyes focused upon Immandra from beneath a pile of wrinkled flesh sagging from her brow. Immandra had never seen anyone more ancient or miserable in all of her life. "Go away. I don't see anybody without an appointment." She turned her back on them and returned to stirring her pot. Her thick, yellowing nails resembled talons, attached to bloated sausage-like fingers with bulbous, swollen knuckles.

"It's important!" Immandra cried out, pleading. "My soulmate, Sian… I must find him and the other adventurers in his party. Please help me. There are many of them and they've gone missing. Their families all seek information as much as I do."

"Hmph. Important for you all, is it, dearie? I couldn't care less. Besides, how much can you pay me? My help is not for free. Return to your village and find payment."

"What about my ring? Surely it would fetch you a fine price." As much as it would hurt to lose the band, gifted on her wedding, it would hurt more to lose Sian and the rest.

Zyda peered over. "It would, sure enough, but it is of little use to me." She spit, her saliva popping in the fire. "Fairy magic. Bah! Take your trinket and bother me no more."

Desperation clawed at Immandra's heart Village. Another vision assaulted her active imagination, and she pictured Sian laying lifeless in the barren fields endlessly stretching before Darknoor Castle. Bleeding and lost to them forever, they would never know the truth.

"Anything!" she finally cried. "I will grant you anything you ask for." How much time would it take her to return to Reindeer Keep to gather a proper payment? And what could the village possibly offer. Panic set her heart to wild thumping in her chest. What if she couldn't afford Zyda's price?

"Oh? Well, in that case, perhaps there is something we could do. And you will not have to return to your village to gather the proper payment after all." Zyda turned and appraisingly ran her dark gaze over the small group. "Your gnome, give him to me. It gets lonesome out here and I could use the company."

"No, no, not that!" Kuiper hastily backed away and ducked behind Immandra's leg. The young woman touched her hand to his head reassuringly.

"Kuiper is a free being. A friend. It is not for me to give him away."

The old crone clucked her tongue. "Pity. It's not a very good start. Not at all." She shook her wrinkled head. "I don't think I can do business with you. You're only wasting my time. I want my payment now for my hard work." She made a shooing gesture with her hand

and resumed her own tedious work.

No! I can't lose like this. Where else will I go if I don't receive aid here? She wondered. It had taken nearly two days to reach her from Kaitan's home, but before that, she had traveled nearly another two days since leaving the village. The time lost and wasted during another roundtrip journey would place Sian's adventure party in greater peril.

"Please, ask me for something else. Give me another chance, I beg of you."

"Hmmn, well then, let me think... Ah. I know what I want." Zyda laughed gleefully. She put her hands on her bony hips and tilted her head back, cackling into the air with delight. "I want to be young and beautiful again. I'll have your body and you can have mine. Hah! What do you say to that, dearie?"

Her body? The thought was so abhorrent that gut instinct almost forced an immediate response from Immandra's lips. Instead, she bit her tongue and stared at the woman. Kuiper tugged on her skirts and pulled until Immandra yielded by backing away from the hut. "I... I have to think about it."

"Don't take too long, dearie. I may just change my mind." Her laughter sent chills trickling down the nape of Immandra's neck.

Immandra retreated from the hut, feeling further from her goal than ever before. Behind her, the laughing crone returned to the task of brewing her alchemical concoction. She hurried away, tears leaking silently down her cheeks. Her steps slowed when she reached the bank of a small creek where she dropped to a seat and buried her face into her hands. Sobs shook her shoulders.

"It's ridiculous!" Kuiper declared. The gnome awkwardly patted the girl on her shoulder with his calloused hands. "How could you think of even changing shapes with that... that horrible, disgusting creature? She stinks!" His nose twitched.

"You can still become Zyda's best friend, Kuiper," Roxy slyly added, looking provocatively at the small man. "Make a little sacrifice for a change."

"No... no..." Immandra swiped at her blotched and wet cheeks. "I would do anything for Sian. But how could I face him wearing Zyda's body? He would never recognize me. He might never love me again."

"No man is worth such a sacrifice." Kuiper crossed his arms and shook his head. "Forget about it and let's go back to the village."

"One of your *wise* suggestions again? Stick to your fishing Kuiper." Roxy swished her tail in agitation.

"If you have a better idea, then let's hear it," the gnome challenged.

"We need Zyda's help. Her price must be paid--"

"How can one think with you two making all this noise?" Immandra spat, fresh tears spilling from her eyes. A merciless ache pulsed between and behind her eyes. On top of her fears of losing her true form, she had a migraine to top it all off. "But Roxy is right... I have no other choice. I must take the witch's offer."

Never in a million years would she have ever guessed that such a fate awaited her the morning she left to visit the still waters of the lake.

If I return home now and tell the Stillwaters the truth, they'll understand. But would I ever forgive myself if I lost this one chance to discover what's happened to

Sian and the others? More than this, her marriage partner was at stake. The welfare and hope of the village relied on his party making a successful adventure to Darknoor and leading the charge against Matta Dora's forces. If the seven adventurers could lead such a dangerous mission, then at the very least, Immandra could contribute her body to the cause.

"I will do it," she decided, standing taller than ever before. "Not only for Sian, but for the rest of Reindeer Keep Village."

***

The hiss and jangle of a rattle made a discordant harmony with the crackling fire and Zyda's guttural, off-tune voice. The witch stood in front of the hearth, shaking the small instrument, while Immandra and her companions watched from the side.

"I have a feeling this will take us nowhere," Kuiper muttered.

Zyda shot the gnome a withered glare. "You are distracting me. Shut up or wait outside."

"Sorry."

"You will be if you say one more word," the witch threatened.

"How long will it take?" Immandra asked, hurrying before Kuiper could open his mouth and make a further mess of things. If she'd been wise, she would have left him outdoors while she conducted her business with Zyda.

"How can one do any work at all with you all blathering on? You want to talk? Fine, let's talk. Forget the ritual."

"Oh no!" Immandra replied swiftly. "No, please, we must go on."

"Then silence!" Zyda's sharp voice made them all wince. "And give me something of Sian's."

Immandra hesitated. Eventually, she reached for a thin leather cord around her neck. She slipped the necklace over her head and gazed down at the small bone pendant with longing. It was once part of the first deer he'd ever slain as a new hunter. As the inhabitants of Reindeer Keep Village were especially close to the wilderness, it was not within their nature to waste any part of the animals that provided their nourishment. He'd skinned the buck and made a fine bag of its hide for Immandra's fifteenth birthday. The bit of bone from his pendant had originated from a rib as a reminder of the day he'd officially become a man among their people. Since Sian had left, she wore it to keep him close. Now, she reluctantly offered it to the witch and wondered if it would be returned.

"Yes, yes, this will do. I must concentrate now and trace him through this." Zyda closed her beady eyes, her face scrunched up. The ancient crone blindly reached for a bowl on the nearby table and thick liquid sloshed within the shallow container. Zyda lifted it to her lips. "I hate this stuff. The things I do for my clients -- I should raise my prices!" Her face twisted as she drank, and then she opened her eyes to cast it aside into the fire. It sent up plumes of purple smoke with an acrid, horrible odor.

The old witch became motionless and her eyes rolled backwards until only the whites showed. She shook and trembled as if in the throes of a horrible possession, until she finally fell back to the floor. After

Zyda struck the ground, Immandra leapt to her feet in alarm to rush over to her. A frown etched deeply into Zyda's face, but she was otherwise motionless as Immandra knelt beside her supine form.

"Seeking... seeking... I have found him... Your young lad is in Darknoor. I see him in darkness. In chains. A prisoner in the clutches of Matta Dora."

"What else can you tell me? Is he alone? Are there others there with him?" Immandra eagerly asked, relieved to know that he continued to live. Imprisonment was a temporary, but reversible state; however, death was permanent.

Zyda became silent upon the ground, stiff as a board. So very still her chest seemed not to move and the air didn't fill her lungs.

Had she died? Immandra looked down, slightly curious, but afraid to touch the woman. "Zyda?"

The silence persisted until finally, the cloudy appearance of the witch's eyes cleared and returned to their usual yellowing and ugly color. Zyda blinked once, twice, then sat up and shook her head. Immandra offered the woman a helping hand up.

"What else did you see, Zyda? Please. Is he okay at least?"

Zyda snorted and shook her head. "He is Matta Dora's new favorite pet. She is trying to break him and make him her lover." The old woman glanced to the younger slyly. "He is not thrilled with the prospect and fights her, but you had best hurry my dear. Once she puts her spell on him, he will be forever lost. Matta Dora is a powerful sorceress."

"Yes, of course." Immandra wrung her hands,

twisting the ring upon her left finger. "And… how do we go about the matter of my payment? Please, let's quickly get it over with so I can get to Sian."

"Ah, but you are a remarkable person, my child." Zyda sighed. For a moment, her features lost their hard lines and unfriendly scowl, until her features softened to an almost cordial countenance. "Your Sian is a lucky man and I… I am beginning to like you a little. So I shall make you a deal."

"What sort of deal?" Alarm bells loudly rang in Immandra's head. She didn't trust this woman, but she didn't wish to trade her youthful shape for a crone's haggard appearance. Sian could never love her then. She couldn't blame him if he felt repulsed from the sight of her. Worse yet, it would ruin their chances of having the family they longed to create one day. Zyda was long past the age for bearing children.

"I will not take your body right away. In fact, you may even keep it so long as you do me one, teensy weensy favor."

"What favor would that be?" Roxy asked from Immandra's shoulder. The little fox's ears stood up straight on her ruddy head.

"Kill Matta Dora for me. I hate that woman and she has crossed me one too many times with her magic." She made it sound easy, like a trivial task no more difficult than squashing a bug. If that were the case, the seven adventurers wouldn't have failed in their task.

Kuiper bristled at Immandra's side. His voice quaked with his anger. "That's not fair! How can we kill the Princess of Darkness?"

Zyda snorted. "Whoever said life was fair? I am

offering the girl a way out of our deal. I will give you thirty days to accomplish your task. You have a full turning of the moon. During that time, we will be changing into each other's form little by little."

"And if I can't kill her? What then?"

"Then I'll enjoy your body for as long as I live. Which will be rather long, I might add. We witches live for a very long time, and with my power I will have a renewed lifespan. You will come grow old and wither away and die within a few years. Pleasing your pretty-faced husband will be the least of your worries." Zyda cackled and turned away from the trio. After a few steps, she turned back. "Oh, and one more thing. To break my spell, Sian must prove he loves you in spite of everything. He must kiss you and mean it."

"And if he doesn't?" Roxy growled.

"Why, then he only loves the girl's body and not her for herself. Who wants that sort of love? You're better off being released from the marriage with your quick and timely death of old age anyway." The witch waved her hand dismissively. "Do you have faith in the love of your marriage, or do you fear he will forsake you?"

"This deal gets worse and worse," Kuiper said. He grumbled and folded his stubby arms against his chest, his sulking features appearing more wrinkled and ugly than ever.

"Come. I will give you a magic wand that will guide you to Darknoor." Zyda rummaged on a shelf then offered out a battered, twisted stick. "Don't lose it. They don't make wands like this anymore. So, do you agree to my terms?"

"I have no choice. What else can I do?"

"What indeed," Zyda chuckled. "The binding ceremony will only take a moment and… it won't hurt."

"Let's get it over with."

Zyda motioned for Immandra to follow her to the back of the room. The old witch drew aside a thick, dark curtain which revealed a hidden alcove. Two cages, much like bird cages, but much larger, stood in the tucked away space. Zyda stepped towards one and motioned Immandra to the other.

"You, little man, you can help by closing the door and fetching the blanket to drape over us. Hurry!"

"Okay, okay." Kuiper reached for a gray cloth draped over the rear of a dingy table, encrusted with a thin layer of grime.

"No! Not that one! The dark one. You're not very bright for a gnome, are you?"

"That's exactly my feeling," Roxy chipped in.

Kuiper's weathered features distorted into another scowl. The thick creases of his forehead nearly drooped over his eyes. "You don't give a gnome a chance, do you? I don't work here! I don't even want to be in this stinkin' place."

"Stinking?" Zyda snarled. "Let me just get my hands on you."

"Peace, please!" Roxy cried. "We have work to do. For Immandra's sake, can we all get along?" Her pleading voice ended the disagreement, coercing Kuiper to silence first. It didn't last for long.

"Alright." Zyda said. "Next time I see you, I'll teach you good manners."

"Over my dead body!"

"That can easily be arranged."

Roxy charged at the gnome and bit his leg. Her small teeth didn't draw blood, but they hurt enough for him to cry out and jerk away from her. He flailed impotently.

"What did you do that for?!"

"We have work to do. We don't have all night. Just do as she says, and shut up!"

Kuiper silenced. He grinded his teeth and threw the dark cloth around Zyda's cage with some difficulty. Too short to accomplish his task on the first try, Kuiper made a second attempt. Darkness fell over Immandra's vision. Her palms grew moist and damp with anticipation, cold dread knotted her belly, and the sound of her own pulse pounded in her ears. She smelled the old hag's scent on the worn cloth, and it took all of her power to remain calm.

She saw nothing and heard nothing, but she felt an electrifying tingle. It fluttered over her body, accompanied by a cooling sensation.

"It's done. You can let us out now. Hurry up. It's hot in here!" Zyda called.

Light flooded the small cage as the blanket came down, revealing the dirty interior of Zyda's hut.

Kuiper shrank away from her. "Oh no…"

Roxy tentatively smelled Immandra from a distance by stretching her neck. The little fox didn't near her immediately. The suspicion filling her furry friend's eyes enveloped Immandra's heart with dread. What had she done to herself?

Zyda rushed to a mirror. Its silver frame no longer gleamed, hidden beneath dust and cobwebs. A spider with a fatly rounded posterior crept from behind the corner of the filthy frame as she swept her sleeve over the opaque layer of grime. It watched Zyda spin and twirl. Although only a few moments had passed, the crone already appeared straighter. The crooked hump of her twisted spine seemed almost normal. Likewise, Immandra felt an ache traveling down her own back. She didn't want to see her face. She couldn't bear it. For the magic to have granted her thirty days of a gradual transition, it had certainly taken a very severe initial toll.

"Well, it wasn't such a bad deal after all. Let's give you some directions before you go. There'll be obstacles along your way."

***

Druid Thorn presided over a meeting around the town's communal fire. People huddled in heavy cloaks and blankets, clutching mugs of warmed cider in their hands. The cold crept in no matter how many layers they wore or how well they tried to insulate their homes. Villagers began sharing their homes simply to generate more body heat in the small spaces.

"The last word we received is that they passed through Gildren's Forge," one of the hunters cried. "Their last riders spoke of smoke over the horizon towards Hazelthorn Mills."

Druid Thorn raised his hands, his expression tired. "Chappeewa has sent word since he left us. Hazelthorn was burned to the ground in a direct assault by Darknoor."

Fearful murmurs and shocked gasps circulated through the crowd. Some people uttered quiet prayers while others spoke curses low beneath their breath.

"More refugees have come in from the outlying homes. They say the cold has killed the wild game, drawing out the wolves," a woman called out.

"What will we do Druid Thorn? Will we survive until the spring? Will it even come?"

"We will do as we have done, and work together," the village elder said, trying to calm their worries. *And we will pray that our forces are enough to face the threat...* He feared for the scouts they sent ahead. He feared if they returned their news would be grim indeed.

"What about Immandra?" one of the women asked. "No one has seen her these past days and no one answers her door."

"She left," a small child answered.

Druid Thorn turned to find the soft-voiced speaker. A young boy crouched close to the fire with his hands extended towards it for the warmth.

"Why didn't you tell us?"

"Imma said she wanted to ask the Fairy Queen about Sian, but she was afraid no one would want her to go if she asked first," the honest child answered.

"Perhaps she is with the fairies then. At least there she'll be safe and comforted."

"Maybe she escaped the village to live with them instead because she knows we're doomed."

"Don't speak about Immandra that way. She wouldn't leave the village like that." The Stillwater patriarch crossed his arms over his chest and glared at the accuser.

"Yes... you're right." The older man heavily sighed and sank back down into his wooden seat. Fears stressed them all, turning neighbor against neighbor during the dire time looming over their community.

"The most we can do then is pray Immandra remains safe," Thorn counseled. "Wherever she may be." *Oh you foolish child. Would you have sought after your husband alone?* Knowing the headstrong girl, he feared it was exactly what she had done. "How go the preparations for battle?"

A thick-muscled man stepped forward from the back. Owen was their blacksmith and had once been a warrior in his prime. He still wielded a blade with proficiency and taught all their hunters and warriors. "We have finished digging a trench around the entire village, three feet deep and twice as wide. Tomas and his workers are busy in his shop as we speak, preparing sharpened spears to place within. I have honed every blade found in the village, be it a sword, axe, or butcher's knife. What ore I have left will be fashioned into basic armor."

"Good... good..." Thorn hoped it was enough. "And our food stores?"

"Dwindling," a woman answered from her seat near the fire. "People are helping as they may, but porridge grows wearisome. The hunters came back with only three rabbits and a single bird this last trip. Not a stag to be seen."

"At least our bellies will be filled, bland though it may be. Let us continue to do what we may and preserve what we have."

"And if our boys do not come home to us?"

The crowd fell into a hush as the question they all wanted to know was finally asked. Solemn faces turned towards the elder and Druid Thorn desperately wished for the words to salve their trepidations.

"Then we have no choice. The men chosen to remain behind must prepare to bear arms against a possible intrusion. We must prepare, as if they have failed in their mission, to rally the army against Darknoor. Failure could mean our demise."

May the Great Mother save us all...

Chapter Eight

THE CURSED BRIDGE

They shortly left the hut after dawn began to approach. The sun continued its downward descent through the sky and the moon climbed steadily higher. Hessop failed to approach Immandra. He suspiciously sniffed her, elongating his neck as Roxy did without daring to shorten the distance between them. Distrust radiated from the intelligent animal.

"He doesn't like the new you," Kuiper determined.

"Hessop, it's me," Immandra said. She reached out with her hand to touch his shaggy, beautiful mane, but he stepped aside to avoid her before her yellowed nails touched his ivory hair.

"Maybe he just doesn't like the smell. I don't care for it either," Roxy said.

"You? Too bad you can't smell yourself. I can catch your stench from miles away," Kuiper retorted.

"Enough!" Immandra shouted in dismay. Tears stung at her eyes. Too stubborn to allow them to fall, she inhaled a deep breath and steeled her nerves. If she wanted to find Sian, she had to be strong. She had to be stronger than the handicap Zyda had forced upon her. "We have to be on our way. I'll kill Matta Dora if I can."

"You better. Or else your body will become mine forever."

"Meanwhile, don't abuse my body. I want to get it back in one piece. Don't wear it out. I have a life to live once I find Sian."

"Then you better hurry, my child." A hopeful glint shined in the woman's milky eyes. "You can always keep my body, you know!"

Cackling, Zyda reentered her humble abode. She practically skipped, enthused with her new acquisition.

With some gentle coaxing, Immandra convinced Hessop to allow her to mount him.

"I think your smell really bothers him, Imma," Roxy spoke up again.

"I can speak for myself," Hessop snapped at last. As a stag of few words, he spoke very little and rarely offered his opinion. He was unlike Roxy and Kuiper, who endlessly bickered and filled every moment of their journey with argument. His silence was welcome. "I needed time to think and to be sure of your identity. The witch has changed you, Immandra, but I see you are not yet Zyda in entirety. What has happened? Why do you wear only part of her visage?" His nostrils flared with each breath, indicating his irritation with the gnome and fox.

"That was the deal," Immandra said quietly. "Her body for mine. I would have paid more though, if it meant finding Sian…"

The mood grew increasingly somber with each passing hour until the silver moon rose high overhead. They settled for a night upon a makeshift camp with spread blankets. Immandra grew a fire into a roaring blaze to drive the chill from their bones. A few hours rest wouldn't hurt their mission.

The formerly young woman awakened with the dawn in pain. She had never experienced the creeping aches of arthritis in her joints and it seemed to pervade her every limb. Kuiper and Roxy looked upon her with sympathetic faces and wisely kept their mouths quiet about her changing appearance. Immandra could only imagine how she looked to them.

Mountainous peaks rose high into the sky, their needled points vanishing into the cloud layer above. The land around them was bare and rocky, sparse with scraggly trees that bent under the wind. The dirt track met at a crossroads and Immandra brought Hessop to a halt. Kuiper startled from his perch in front of her on the saddle and Roxy sleepily peeked out from her pocket.

The paths were exactly as Zyda had warned. "The wand doesn't work here in the shadow of the Devil's Crest," Immandra said tiredly. Her voice croaked, sounding aged to even her own ears. She cringed and took a hasty sip of water from her nearly empty canteen. Resources had become scarce and their supplies had dwindled to practically nothing. Kuiper ate far too much despite his tiny size.

"But there are five paths! Which way?" Roxy bristled.

A metal plaque embedded in the way marker offered little help. They gathered around it and studied the worn writing with grim expressions.

"All this says is death, death, and more death," Kuiper fussed. "Only one safe path it says, but not a clue as to which."

"It's been rubbed away by the elements." Immandra rubbed her fingers against her temple. Her pulse pounded behind her eyes and her vision dizzily swam for a moment. "This place feels strange. I need to think." She turned away from the stone marker and started to pull supplies from Hessop's saddlebags.

"Good idea, making camp. I'm starved." Kuiper scrambled across the ground and began to collect dry twigs and sticks for a fire.

"Of course," Roxy snorted. "That's all you ever think of, Kuiper. Eat. Eat. Eat."

"Enough!" Immandra's voice echoed sharply across the wasteland. "I'm trying to *think* and all you two can do is snipe at one another. All you ever do is fight. Enough."

They made camp in subdued silence. Their small campfire provided warmth, but did little to cheer them. Not even a pot of stew brightened Immandra's aging features. She sat with her eyes downcast, twisting the ring the fairy queen gifted her around and around on her finger. The changes showed in her wrinkled hands and yellowing nails.

"What if we choose wrong?" Her quiet question broke the tense silence between the three companions.

"You worry too much." Roxy slunk closer and leaned into Immandra's leg. The fox rubbed her rusty head against the young woman's calves.

"The fox is right. Your journey requires confidence,

and your worries will be the death of you. Proceed with wisdom, Immandra," Hessop said. "Know that I will bear you whichever way you desire."

"What about the fairy ring?" Kuiper's eyes brightened and he pointed at the bit of jewelry. "Can we use it to call for help?"

"I'd almost forgotten about it... Of course. Lady Sibba said I would find aid with its use."

"See? I have good ideas sometimes." Kuiper puffed his chest.

Roxy chuffed. "Once every few hundred years or so. Nothing to gloat about."

"Enough you two. No more bickering. Now be quiet and let me concentrate."

Immandra closed her eyes and held her hand over her heart. Her brow crinkled and she desperately wished for help from someone. Anyone.

Nothing happened.

No magic gleamed from the piece of jewelry. No warmth bloomed between her hands. No help came.

"My heart it too troubled," Immandra said, her shoulders slumping. "It won't respond if I have dark feelings."

"Then let's rest. A good night's sleep will make you feel better." Roxy hopped into Immandra's lap and curled up.

They all settled in close to Hessop for warmth, sharing their meager blanket. The large riding animal's body heat felt good to Immandra's aching bones.

***

The morning's dismal gray skies created a depressing atmosphere. It didn't lift their somber moods. Immandra awakened to hear bickering between Roxy and Kuiper over their dwindling food reserves.

"You eat everything," Roxy complained.

"Maybe if I stuffed some more food in your mouth you would talk less," Kuiper retorted.

Immandra ignored them in favor of trying the ring's powers again. As it had the night before, no magic flared to life from the gift.

"Let me have a look," Kuiper said, taking the ring from her.

"I don't think shaking it will help." Immandra shook her head, hands on her hips, and watched the gnome jostle the ring around in his hand. If anything, she worried he would damage the trinket. She quickly snatched it back before any harm could be done.

"I don't know much about fairy magic," Kuiper admitted.

"You don't know much about anything," Roxy shot back at him.

"*Don't* you start that now," Immandra interrupted them sharply. "We're short on time."

"We're also going to see a blizzard today," Roxy said. The fox turned her nose toward the air, as if she could scent the snow in the breeze, winding between the sparse trees.

"All the more reason to get moving. But this ring won't work!"

"Wait. Didn't Lady Sibba say your heart had to be full of love?" Kuiper pointed out. "Try to think of something pleasant."

"I don't feel particularly loving at this very moment." She gave Kuiper and Roxy a pointed look. Abashed, Kuiper looked at his own two feet.

"Sorry," he apologized. "Can you try to think of something pleasant?"

"Nothing pleasant comes to mind. Not too surprising, all things considered."

"What about Sian? Think about him," Roxy suggested helpfully.

If not for Sian, Immandra would never have left the village. She'd be at home safe and warm by the fire, holding a hot cup of cocoa and dreaming of their future together as husband and wife. If not for Matta Dora, she and Sian might have broached the subject of raising children and living happily ever after.

Immandra couldn't have her happily ever after until she found him and brought him safely home. And to do that, she had to kill Matta Dora. She had to prove to Zyda that he still loved her, through and through, regardless of her exterior appearance. Within seconds, her love for Sian flooded her emotions. Immandra's hopes surged with warmth.

The ring exploded with a bright inner glow, washing the three with golden light.

"Call for help!" Kuiper shouted. He rubbed his hands together eagerly and clapped.

"Hear me, all creatures, big and small! I need your help…"

Nothing happened at first. The glow continued, lively pulsing and hot in her hands. Gradually, a few birds began to drop from the sky and land upon nearby tree limbs. A small songbird touched down on

Immandra's extended arm. A rabbit leapt up from behind the rocks as a large crow landed heavily upon her left shoulder..

"Wow!" Kuiper cried.

"Tell me, little brothers. How can I find the way to Darknoor?"

The black crow swung his head around and briefly shuffled in place. Then he took off with a noisy caw. "Follow me! I'll show you the way to Darknoor Castle."

"Looks like we have a guide," Kuiper said. "It wasn't too hard, was it?"

"To master dark emotions is not an easy thing. When you turn to love, all things are possible," Roxy spoke up thoughtfully.

"I never thought I would hear that from your lips. Why don't you try to live up to those principles?"

"I am a very loving being," Roxy argued.

"I've never noticed that."

"Come on," Immandra interrupted them. She sighed and shook her head, but a faint hint of a smile crept over her lips. With love, all things were possible. And with love, she would be led to Sian to save him.

Hessop finished scraping the ground for errant bits of green grass and clover amid the rocky terrain. The group gathered their belongings and returned to the trail with their crow guide in the lead.

They reached a river by midday and followed its banks for a time. Try as they might, their wandering alongside the river failed to yield a safe passage to cross. The wide channel of water flowed strong and fast, with choppy waves breaking against jagged rocks that peeked up from below. It would be suicide to test their strength against the river's fury.

Fortunately, they discovered a bridge after another mile. The stone and wooden structure arched over the deep waters. Moss clung to the weathered stone and darkened the wood. At its highest point, in the very middle, a swirl of ominous fog hung in the air. The thick cloud obscured the pathway for several feet and brought their group to a swift halt to warily investigate the path ahead.

"The River Garron..." Roxy whispered tremulously.

"I've heard tales about this bridge," Immandra replied with equal quiet. "My nurse told me that long ago, Wizard Barmakian cursed it. Since then, no one has ever crossed the bridge alive. The dark force guarding it kills all who make the attempt."

"But why?" Kuiper asked. He fidgeted in his seat and held Hessop's mane with a white-knuckled grip. Immandra kissed the top of his head to ease his fear.

"No one knows." Roxy replied. "But there's a prophecy that says one day someone pure of heart will come and break the spell."

"And nobody's succeeded so far?" Kuiper shook his head. "Nope. I'm not going anywhere near that bridge. Not going to do it."

"I really don't envy your cowardly character." Roxy swished her tail. "It must be hard to live with."

"Not nearly as hard as living with your charming self," Kuiper retorted.

Roxy opened her mouth to argue, but she paused and seemed to realize Immandra had become too stressed to bear the burden of their bickering. The white fox silenced and simply turned her face aside instead.

Immandra flashed a grateful, but tiny smile. "Roxy, why don't you go to find us some eggs for dinner. And you, Kuiper, find some dry wood to make a fire." She rubbed her hands together. Her fingernails had practically begun to yellow overnight, and the joints of each digit ached with the arrival of the cold.

Thankfully, Immandra hadn't seen her own reflection in quite a while, but the physical changes she experienced in her body were enough to make her dread seeing her appearance. She needed to find Sian and fast, while some youthful vitality still remained in her bones. With Kuiper's aid, she managed to gather enough dry wood and start a small campfire.

Roxy returned with eggs and a few edible mushrooms. By then, Immandra had settled near the fire to begin counting knots on a string. It was her only method of keeping track of the passing days since leaving Zyda's hut.

"How long has it been?" Roxy asked.

"Seven days tonight. Time is running fast. We shall cross tomorrow."

Hessop cast a nervous, fearful look towards the bridge. The large animal had found a few bits of frozen grass after scraping his hooves against the snow. He snorted warm steam, but seemed to accept her declaration.

"I do not like the site of this bridge. It is an evil place filled with despair and suffering. Many have lost their lives, many succumbed to the darkness," Hessop rumbled in his deep voice.

"This is the only safe way to Darknoor, so we'll have to do it," Kuiper said.

"It's waiting to devour us. How can we defeat something like this?" Immandra asked, agreeing with Hessop.

"There must be a way," Roxy stated. "Could the ring protect us?"

"I don't know. There's only one way to find out," Immandra replied.

Immandra wiped her hands against her skirt to reduce the sweat. Hessop's braided lead had begun to dig into her palms, held by an overtight grip. The horned animal had no more desire to attempt crossing than she did, but they needed to get across. Roxy quivered in Immandra's pocket and Kuiper grabbed the woman's other hand.

"Get a firm grip on your emotions," Roxy encouraged. "No trace of negativity can blemish your thoughts. You did so well last time."

The supportive warmth of her friends helped Immandra greatly. She sucked in a deep breath and nodded her head in response.

"I know what to do. Get in my pocket, Roxy. I'll protect you."

Roxy scrambled into Immandra's pocket. Only the tip of her nose, pointed ears, and two shining eyes remained visible. Immandra resumed holding Hessop's rein in one hand. Kuiper held the other.

"May the Lady and the Forces of Light protect us."

The sun-bleached bones of many different creatures littered the stone arch. Most held the yellowed color of age, but a few looked fresh. Bits of decaying flesh still clung to the white skulls.

A dark presence stirred in the middle of the bridge.

Ghastly faces coalesced in the fog and horrible, demonic features became apparent to Immandra's vision. The terrifying sight made a breath catch in her throat. Her steps briefly faltered, but Kuiper's hold on her hand tightened. He instinctively flinched back and to her rear, Hessop stopped moving.

"We are not alone, Immandra," Hessop said.

"We can do this," she whispered. Her determination grew, overcome with rising courage. A tug of Hessop's reins drew him to follow her steps.

Electricity crackled in the air and danced on the wind. It stirred Immandra's dark hair, lifting the silken strands over her head. The faces in the darkness gnashed their teeth and reached out with clawed hands. Despite her terror, Immandra pushed forward against the unforgiving winds. They were turbulent and cruel. Occasionally, a pebble or some small object whipped past her face and nicked the skin. One left a small gash on her cheek.

The swirling fog enveloped them. Kuiper grasped her sleeve in despair when a demonic mouth snapped inches away from his ear. A ghoulish hand snapped out and clamped around Immandra's throat. Her scream never formed, her air cut off by the tight squeeze.

"Let her go! You let her go!" Kuiper batted the spectral arms to no avail. His fingers passed through the ghostly substances causing Immandra harm. The world around her swam and darkened, casting black spots in her vision. She fought against the loss of consciousness, the cold sensation spreading throughout her limbs, and the powerful force seeking to overtake her. An evil, malevolent presence seized Immandra's hands.

"The wand, the wand!" Roxy squealed from Immandra's pocket. She nosed around in the woman's garments, nudging the gnarled stick out. Kuiper grasped hold of it and brandished the magical tool at the shadows. It sparked at the tip, but did little else. When the magic of the wand failed Kuiper, he wedged it between the claws and Immandra's throat. Mystical energy seemed better suited at parting them than his tiny fingers. The shadows lunged backwards and dispersed. Immandra dropped to the ground with wheezing gasps.

"Your ring, Immandra. Use the ring!" Hessop cried in terror to her rear.

Immandra had no idea if it would work. The ring was supposed to bring her aid, but it was an item crafted from fairy magic. She pressed the ring to her heart and cried out for help. "Mother! We need your help!" Roxy and Kuiper continued to help. "Hurry up!" Roxy screamed.

"It's not working!"

"You know what to do. Think of Sian for heaven's sake! Think of Sian!"

Sian's face easily came to her thoughts. The warmth of his embrace and the memory of his sweet kisses renewed Immandra's strength. It seemed like only yesterday that they were wed within the center of the village as husband and wife.

"It's working!" Roxy shouted joyously.

I have to bring him home, Immandra thought. Determined, she applied her willpower against the insidious force. The pressure edged in against her vision again, as if the thought of Sian alone weren't enough to abolish the sinister curse. "I won't.... I won't let you win!" she cried out in triumph. She thought of Roxy and Kuiper. They were counting on her as well. Surely, if she fell and succumbed to the dark forces, her friends would be next. For the first time since the start of her adventure, more than Sian counted on her. Roxy and Kuiper's lives depended upon her success. Behind her, Hessop laboriously breathed and made strained noises.

Heat exploded from the ring. The sensation was molten hot, burning in a way that transcended actual physical pain. It was a fire of the senses and the spirit only. It mercilessly crashed against the demon inhabiting the bridge and dislodged its grip. The claws withdrew as the fairy magic banished the fog's cruel inhabitants. Immandra was freed. She felt overcome with joy as the misty cloud continued to recede, but her heart sank in dismay when she realized Kuiper was nowhere in sight.

"Kuiper?" Immandra called uncertainly.

"Down there!" Roxy leapt to the ground to land beside the gnome's prostrated body. He lay too still for their liking.

"He's hardly breathing," Immandra muttered. During her efforts to rouse him from his stupor, she slapped his face less gently than intended

"Kuiper, please wake up!"

Kuiper's pale cheeks lacked their usual ruddy glow and even the bald plate of his skull seemed as white as the bones littering the bridge. Immandra's heart fearfully pounded at the thought of losing her companion. In that moment, she prayed harder than she'd ever had to pray before, pleading to any being in the heavens above willing to answer her pleas.

It turned out, they only needed Roxy. She bit him

sharply on the hand and the startled gnome awakened with a scream. He jerked upright, looking around wildly and clutching his wounded hand to his chest. Tiny toothmarks imprinted his skin, but at least his color had begun to return.

"Kuiper!" Immandra hugged him tightly against her and wept against the top of his head. How could she have ever found happiness with Sian if she lost her friends along the way?

"You let her try to eat me!"

"I worried about you, you fool!"

For the first time in a long while of their travels, Immandra didn't care about Roxy and Kuiper's bickering. She only laughed and hugged him even tighter. Crushed, Kuiper squeaked in protest when the formidable strength of her larger body squished the air from his lungs. As if to convey his gratitude, Hessop nudged Immandra's shoulder from behind with his antlered head.

They were all alive. She'd saved all of them.

"We did it," she whispered. Her gaze moved to the cleared bridge. Already the sun seemed to shine more brightly, warming the stone. No trace of the cursed aura remained.

"Now travelers can come and go in safety," Kuiper said in quiet awe. No one else would ever fall prey to the malevolent spirit of the cursed bridge.

"I say this deserves a celebration. And a well-deserved rest." Roxy swished her tail.

"I'll catch us some fish!" Kuiper hurried up the river bank, intent on his goal.

Roxy and Immandra made camp while Hessop eagerly foraged by scraping his hoof against the snowy ground. He seemed drained, following their trial at the bridge, and eager to search for an acceptable meal. Immandra mourned that she had nothing better to offer him than the occasional oat biscuit from her dwindling supply of rations.

"Are you not hungry for more?" she asked him, concern furrowing her brow. She often feared that her friends were not acquiring enough nourishment. During their travels, Immandra had lost the ability to determine if her own loosening clothing came as a result of poor eating habits or her gradual transition to Zyda's body.

"I will survive," Hessop told her. He lowered his head to the ground again and nosed aside a small amount of slush. "We are bred for this weather and to tolerate distant travel. All my kind in the mountains are known for this. Your adventure has harmed me none, and I may travel for a greater distance yet. Worry not for me, young fey-child."

"What are you?" she asked curiously. "I am not familiar with the mountains or much of these lands outside of Reindeer Keep Village. The rest of Sinead is a wonder to me."

"We are snow deer, larger and hardier than our cousins of the forest. We make our home in the mountains where the snow is lasting. The genie Kaitan Speedwell is a friend to our people. He has protected us many times from our enemies and those who would see us as prey." He raised his face from the cold grass and Immandra received the impression that the creature was smiling. "It is an honor to help you at his behest."

"Thank you just the same, Hessop," Immandra told him.

Hessop may have claimed that he needed nothing more from her, but Immandra spent the next few moments using the side of her shoe to discover fresh patches of frosted grass. It would make a tasty treat after the scraggly weeds on the other side of the river.

***

"Sian, you're supposed to be good with your hands. Can't you get out of those irons?"

"With what? Am I supposed to pick them with straw?"

The three men sat in their filthy cell, grimy and covered with sweat. Due to the arrival of a frigid winter season, the warmed dungeons became a blessing at times. At others, the unbearable heat drove them closer to dehydration until they were parched for water. They received very little of that, resulting in Yorteze suffering the most. His wilted appearance led to Sian sacrificing his single tin cup of water for the sylvan. His woody skin dulled and became gray in places, wrinkled like an overripe piece of shriveling fruit.

In exchange for that bit of sacrificed water, Yorteze managed to coax nutritious plant matter and lichen to grow between the cracks of the dungeon's foundation. They eagerly gobbled the tasteless food, starved for anything at all besides the thin gruel brought by the castle's dungeon master.

"You could have gone free and I... I couldn't do it."

"Do you truly believe she would have let us go?" Yorteze asked in his low voice. "No. Her idea of freedom likely meant another cell or a painful death."

"Or maybe she would have really let us go," Gibber snapped.

"I don't believe her," Sian spoke up softly. "It's most likely she'll slit your throats the moment I'm no longer here among you, and I won't do that to any of you. I won't leave you here to die and I won't be untrue to Immandra either. I couldn't live with myself if..." Sian shook his head.

"Do you think that pretty wife of yours wants you to die down here instead?"

"I'm sorry, Giber, but I just can't do it."

Giber sighed and nodded his head in defeat. "I know, Sian. It felt wrong to even ask you to do it anyway. It was a stupid thing to say."

Uneasy silence came between them again. Yorteze broke it first.

"Do you believe the girl-child made it to the village?"

"I hope so," Sian muttered. He glanced towards his wrist at the iron secured to the wall. The stone masonry appeared old, crumbling from age and wear. "Yorteze."

The sylvan raised his head with a dry croak. "Yes?"

"Hand me back my cup. I have an idea."

The sylvan's shaky hand barely delivered the cup to him. Sian used the edge of it to scrape at the weak chunks of mortar. Pebbled pieces broke away little by little. He planned to pull the chain out of the wall to free his hand.

It worked like a charm while the dungeon master's apprentice snoozed at a nearby desk, his cheek against the grimy wood. He stirred once, but lapsed back into a deep slumber after several moments of renewed silence.

Sian breathed his relief and began to tug at the chain until the remaining stone around it gave and it pulled free completely.

"By the gods, he's done it," Giber said.

Once he had a hand free, the rest came easily.

"You probably could have done it with a piece of straw," Giber grumbled.

Sian grinned at him, feeling more upbeat about their situation than he'd felt in days. "Probably could have. I just needed my hands free. There wasn't enough slack in the chain before.

"Do you think you can get the lock on the door? We can make a grab for some weapons, try to escape," Giber suggested.

Yorteze said nothing at all to them, his despondent appearance quickly taking the wind from Sian's sails. The sylvan's lifeless eyes focused beyond the cell bars, appearing to see nothing. He had to conserve his energy for battle.

"And what about all these other people," Sian argued. The dungeons overflowed with victims and prisoners, the survivors of the attack on Hazelthorn Forge. "We can't just leave them."

"If we get out of here," Giber countered in a rough whisper, "we can bring back the army and save all their wretched hides."

"Junua will bring the army."

"If she escaped. For all we know her corpse was picked clean by the Doom Fliers. Can we really leave it to chance?"

"Giber has a point, youngling. We cannot depend upon her to bring the army, no more than we can free each man in these cells. We must fly with haste and gain our own freedom for now." Yorteze spoke with a saddened voice, the angst apparent in his features. The weight of his own words seemed too heavy on his spirits and the truth became a bitter pill to swallow. If they wanted to save the many, they would have to leave without them.

"I don't have to like it."

"Live a little longer, Sian. You will understand one day," Yorteze told him.

Sian silenced to avoid arguing with his three cell mates and battle companions. Giber had suffered enough and had sufficient reason for looking out for his own tail. Their sylvan friend was at death's door.

"Keep an eye on the guard," Sian muttered. He crouched down near the door of their cell and took a look at the large lock. The heavy iron showed signs of wear and rust, but looked solid. Without a weapon to break it, he was left with finding a way to pick it.

"What about this?" Giber asked, rummaging on the cell floor. "It's only a splinter of metal, but maybe it will do?"

"Pass it over."

The minutes ticked by, but the audible snick of the lock eventually rewarded Sian's efforts. The trio crept from their cell, eyes alert and stances wary.

"Take us with you!" a desperate man cried from a neighboring cell.

"Shhh!" Giber hissed back. "You'll wake the guard and get us all killed!"

"Too late," Yorteze warned.

Beneath the flickering light of a torch, the dungeon

master's lone apprentice occupied a seat at a desk near the wall. He swiftly rose, drawing his sword from the scabbard in a fluid stroke.

Armed with only the wrist irons from his cell, Sian dashed forward and swung the heavy circle of metal by its chain. The improvised weapon struck the first guard in his unprotected cheek, cracking the bone beneath. The man stumbled backward, but he had no chance to recover. Giber was upon him quickly afterward to mercilessly slam the back of his skull against the wall. Their freedom relied upon clearing the way as swiftly as possible.

To prevent the jangling of their chains, they relieved the guard of his clothing and tore it into strips. The material easily muffled the heavy irons and ceased the heavy clanking of each link.

"Take his weapon, Giber. I'm fine with these."

"You're better with a chain than I am," the burly warrior agreed.

Sian weakly grinned at the other man. As the healthiest and least injured of the three men, he led Yorteze and Giber through the darkened castle corridors. Exhaustion and malnourishment had dulled Giber's reflexes and battle skills. He lingered to the rear of the group once Yorteze assured them he could still manipulate his powers. Whether it was by his youthful stamina or Matta Dora's favoritism, Sian remained in better health.

The dank underground tunnels smelled sour, heavy with death and despair. Sian tried not to think too heavily about the smells and their sources. They wound their way upwards almost blindly, searching their dwindling memories of the fortress and sometimes bickering to decide their course.

"I am telling you, Sian. It's this way."

"You're half delirious with hunger and you're wanting us to trust your memory?" Sian asked incredulously. Yorteze's dry chuckle resembled the noise of twigs scraping over bark.

"Over here. We'll exit the dungeons into the servant's quarters this way," Sian whispered. Their surroundings became too still and quiet, suspiciously noiseless and without interference. The hairs on the back of Sian's neck prickled. Something felt wrong. Without a guard in sight to stop them, it felt too easy.

When taken captive, the soldiers stripped them of all weapons and armor. They crept barefoot, which proved to be to their advantage. They overheard a pair of soldiers playing cards and aimlessly chatting about their everyday activities, but easily snuck past them to the rear and remained unseen.

"I smell a breeze, cold and clean," Yorteze rumbled quietly. "This way."

"I'd settle for a window at this point." Giber grunted. "Anything to get us out of here."

Wide stairs led them up to the next level and into the servants' quarters as predicted. A second door led into a wide washing room. Metal tubs lined the walls and were filled with laundry, but not a single servant lurked anywhere in the room. They continued through more narrow halls, following Yorteze's nose.

The next door opened into a large receiving chamber. Crimson velvet drapes framed towering windows and were drawn back to allow in the light.

After days spent in the dungeons, the illumination blinded them.

It was a trap.

"Get them!"

The hounds reached them first. Blood shone upon their brindle coats and gore clung to yellowed teeth. Yorteze kicked out at the first, slamming the snarling animal against the wall. It yelped, bones cracking. The second snapped at Giber and Sian, attempting to drive them back.

Sian whipped his improvised chain at the hound's snout. Bright red blood welled up against its muzzle and it turned its burning eyes on him. If he hadn't already faced a Doom Flier face to face, he might have been terrified.

"Back you rabid mongrel!" He slammed the manacles down again and again. A furry ear ripped free and the animal fled, whimpering and whining.

It did no good when more of her men awaited them. Once the dogs were gone, it quickly became apparent that their path remained obscured. Nearly two dozen guards waited, each anonymous face concealed by macabre helms fashioned into ghoulish expressions. They were her best soldiers, the elite officers who personally served at her beck and call.

Matta Dora's squad of well-trained soldiers moved forward in perfect harmony. With their shields raised, their defense became impregnable, and no amount of swinging from his manages broke through the wall of moving guards.

A shield struck Sian's ribcage. It drove the wind from his lungs and shoved him back.

"You've heard the orders from the mistress! Cause no permanent harm to the pretty one. The others are to be killed at will for standing against us."

"No!" Sian cried. "There's too many! Fall back, we must find another way!"

"Too late!" Yorteze bellowed.

Men with spears and others with crossbows spilled into the passageway behind them, boxing the trio in. With nowhere left to go, they lowered their weapons.

So close! Sian thought in despair. To come so far and fail at the last minute seemed like the cruelest fate.

"Did you really think I would let you escape?"

Matta Dora stepped into view, the hulking form of General Stern behind her. Sian's vision wavered, fading in and out.

"I hope you enjoyed your pitiful attempt and realize now that you have no power. No chance for escape." She crouched down and tipped Sian's bloody chin up with a single finger. "You. Are. Mine."

Darkness pulled him under.

***

Another week of travel brought them through the mountains to rolling foothills. Immandra had taken to carrying Zyda's wand in her hands at all times. She wanted to be prepared for the inevitable trouble to be found around every turn. She never failed to do so, even if it became increasingly difficult to grip the magical wand in her hands. Her swollen joints protested holding anything at all.

By now, Hessop, Kuiper, and Roxy had adjusted to her ever changing appearance and no longer commented about her poor looks. Sensing her despair and nonexistent self-esteem, the trio of animal friends often changed the subject by drawing her attention to the winter scenery or some other aspect of their journey.

No amount of distraction would change the transformation ravaging her body or that she knew it was happening. Immandra's beautiful hair had become coarse, dull, and thin, falling lank to frame either side of her face. Aged creases formed at the corners of her mouth. Her clothing loosely hung where voluptuous curves had once filled out the bodice of her dress.

"I smell a fire," Roxy commented. "Smells like a wood furnace. Someone must live nearby."

Hessop snorted and continued to amble along at his sedate pace, never rushing, but never slowing. "Am I to take us to the sound, Immandra?"

"Maybe it's someone who can help us… we're almost out of food and I think we're all tired of fish," she replied. The stag glanced back at her over his muscled shoulder.

"I am fortunate. I do not consume your fish, but I tire of watching you eat it," he commented.

"I tire of watching Kuiper catch it," Roxy said.

"Hey! What's wrong with fish? Fish is perfect at all times of the day, every day of the year. You can't go wrong with fish," Kuiper argued hotly. They had wounded him down to his core with their dismissal of the importance of fish in a daily diet.

Immandra chuckled despite the severity of their situation. It would be nice to receive the aid of another person. "Yes, let's go there, Hessop. I have some things to offer in trade."

A repetitious thud reached their ears before they spotted the hut. A man chopped wood outside the small and humble structure. The breeze ruffled his wispy gray hair and the sun highlighted his sun-weathered skin. Despite his aged appearance, he swung his axe with strength and precision.

The old man looked up when they rode into view. He lifted his hand to shade his face against the sun, eyes widening. "You!" His deep voice easily reached them. "You dare to come *here*, after all you've done?"

Immandra drew Hessop to a halt. Her fingers tightened around the wand in her hand. "What have I done?" she called back in confusion. She lowered from Hessop's back with care. Lately, her curving spine had begun to take a toll on her movements. She no longer felt the spry freedom of youth and struggled to continue the usual day-to-day activities of travel.

How could she possibly succeed in her mission with Zyda's traitorous body as her tool?

"Don't you dare play dumb with me, Zyda Bitternel! You deprived me of my honor, my pride, my... everything!"

"What? But I'm not Zyda--"

"I was hoping someday I would meet you again. Repay you..," the man continued on in a heated tone. "Repay you for all the humiliation I've suffered".

"She's not Zyda," Kuiper finally shouted. His indignation touched Immandra and brought a tiny smile to her face.

"Daft human, she speaks only the truth to you," Hessop argued for her.

"And you just come here asking for punishment."

The embittered man clearly didn't have any desire to listen to them. Their words went in one ear and out the other, completely ignored. "It's my lucky day!" he cried triumphantly. He thrust his hand into his pocket and came up with a handful of old-tattered string. The threads appeared fragile, but after he uttered a single incantation he cast it at her. It came to life as a monstrous serpent composed of living fire. It winded around her from the knees to the shoulders in a constrictive embrace.

Intense heat swam over Immandra's body and blisters arose wherever it made contact. It singed through her clothing and practically lit her entire body aflame. She screeched in agony and arched her back. The wand simply tumbled from her fingers.

"This is a mistake!" Immandra shrieked in pain. "I only look like her! Stop! Please!"

The cackling wizard shook his head. "I can't believe my luck!" he crowed victoriously. Her words fell on deaf ears. Kuiper tried to pluck at one of the bonds around her knee level. He jerked his hand away and swore a gnomish curse.

"Please, it hurts!"

Roxy leapt from atop Hessop's back. "She really isn't Zyda! She's Immandra Stillwater of Reindeer Keep Village! You're making a mistake," the little fox cried out to him. Immandra writhed in agony, her clothing continuously consumed by the fire that raged around her. The flame licked at her hair.

"Are you by any chance Tarr Nettlewort of Raven Hills? The famous wizard?" Kuiper asked desperately.

"The very same. Flattery, however, will get you

nowhere. Your mistress and I are sworn enemies," Tarr replied.

"But--"

"Stay out of this!" Tarr roared at Kuiper. A snap of his fingers created a crashing wall of wind. It tossed Kuiper into the air and carried the small gnome away from them. He struck a tree and fell to the ground motionless.

"Please! I'm not the person you want!" Immandra was reduced to tears. She sobbed and twisted. Her futile movements did nothing to aid her and only exposed more of her flesh to the spell's branding heat. "Please don't hurt him!"

"Of course you are. Why else would you be sneaking up on me like that? Do you have any new tricks in store for me, you flea bitten hag? I must warn you, I already know most of them."

There must be some way out of this, Immandra thought. Relief overwhelmed her when Kuiper finally began to stir and climb to his feet.

"You really do have the wrong person! Immandra isn't Zyda," Roxy said. "You have to believe us."

"I don't want to hear one more word. You've gotten exactly what you deserve, witch." He snapped and the flames extinguished. Immandra's relieved sobs failed to move him. "I'll figure out what to do with you by morn. Try to escape, or if your friends try to free your binds, the flames will come back even hotter."

Tarr ignored the rest of their weakening pleas. He turned his back on the group and strode away.

"Immandra, Immandra..." Kuiper patted at her tear soaked cheeks and Roxy gently sniffed at her burns.

"What shall we do?"

"She needs healing or it will all scar," Hessop said.

"What does it matter?" Immandra cried. "What are scars when I look like this? Like Zyda."

The larger creature lowered his head to inspect her thoroughly. "I could try to remove them with my antlers. The fire will not harm them."

"You can't give up hope, not now," Roxy squealed. "Oh I wish I knew what to do."

Kuiper wrung his stumpy hands. "I may have an idea..."

"What idea, Kuiper?"

He looked up into Immandra's pained face. "Sing. I heard you once, when you sang for Sian on the hill. It was beautiful. No one as wicked as Zyda could sing something so touching. So... sing for the wizard Tarr. He'll have to realize his mistake then."

"That's brilliant, Kuiper." Roxy said in awe. "I think it could work."

"The gnome is on to something. Sing your most beautiful song, Immandra. Perhaps it will become a balm to his embittered heart and he will see through Zyda's spell," Hessop urged her.

"Then... then I'll try. Perhaps a song will soften his heart."

In her desperation, she was willing to try almost anything if it meant she'd be given the freedom to resume her quest. For Sian, she had no choice but to push through and to escape her own imprisonment.

She began with a hum when Tarr came into view again. He wielded an axe to resume chopping his wood, but she feared her singing wouldn't carry the distance to reach him. Her screams and cries of agony had strained her voice.

I must. If I can't escape this, I can't help Sian. What will become of my friends if I die in captivity? Her voice became stronger. Through sheer willpower and determination, Immandra's voice bloomed to fill the entire meadow.

Will my love survive the trials?
Is it strong enough to last?
Ask the tree
Ask the sky
Ask whoever pass you by.

Will my Sian still love me changed
Beauty gone and looking strange?
Ask the lake
Ask the grass
Ask whoever you may pass.

Will my love be still so strong
To make a fairy stone ring glow?
Ask the fox
Ask the crow
Ask all things that live and grow.

Will my love still warm my heart
Lost in blizzard, low my guard?
Ask the frost
Ask the ice
Ask those things that shine so nice.

Will my love still magic make?
Will I know to give or take?
Ask the wand
Cast the spell
You will ring the magic bell.

"See! She's not Zyda," Kuiper called out again. "Now please release her, we must be on our way to Darknoor."

Tarr had been moved to tears. Moisture trails glistened upon the old man's weathered cheeks. He stood near the pile of split wood, no longer holding his axe. The tool lay on the ground beside his foot instead. "Not Zyda? To Darknoor?" He seemed bewildered and confused by his grave mistake. "Who the hell are you? Isn't this only another of your unpleasant tricks, Zyda Bitternell?"

"I'm Immandra Stillwater of Sinead, on a quest to find my soulmate. Sian has been taken prisoner in Darknoor. Now will you please take this awful thing off of me?"

Tarr chuckled. The dry, humorless sound grated Immandra's nerves, but she bit her tongue and waited with all of the patience she could muster. When Tarr whispered the counterspell to his curse, the ropes simply fell away as tattered bits of broken string. "I'm sorry. I had to take precautions. Zyda has played one trick too many."

"It would be easy to forgive, but for these burns…"

"Oh Immandra, your hair," Roxy said mournfully.

"It isn't the hair that bothers me. It was Zyda's hair anyway," Immandra said. Her clothing had been ruined, reduced to singed rags. The wrinkled skin, revealed through the ashen bits of material, sagged and hung. She modestly wrapped her arms around her aging body, too ashamed to let anyone see it. "But these burns are real for me, and they hurt."

"Come. I'll give you salve to put on them. You'll be as good as new tomorrow."

By the next morning, Immandra felt marked improvement. Maybe that had something to do with sleeping in a warm bed, since the wizard had sacrificed his own mattress and comforts of home to allow her a peaceful night's rest. Roxy and Kuiper slept near. Hessop nestled outside next to the wizard's equine mount beneath a suitable shelter of wood and thatch.

Immandra awakened to a folded lump of cloth upon the foot of the bed. It was suspiciously similar to her body's size, plain, but warm for the current weather. Tarr also replenished their rations and supplies by providing dried fruits, meats, and vegetables able to endure the long journey. Wrapped loaves of traveler's bread and crackers completed his gift. He refilled their empty canteens with sweet stream water with a fragrant taste.

"It's not water," he grumpily corrected Immandra when she asked. "It's my special Yinwao tea. It'll help you on your travels."

Her joints felt oddly warm. The liquid within the wooden mug was practically translucent with only a hint of a green tint. She sniffed again.

"My pain is gone!"

"That it is. I wish I could go with you to Darknoor. I have a score to settle with Mizar Thunderstone... but I'm too old."

"*Everybody* has a score to settle with that guy. I'm beginning to understand why Darknoor has such a bad reputation," Kuiper grumped.

"Indeed," Tarr replied. He glanced over a shoulder toward a heavy, wooden chest with several buckles and locks without holes for keys. His eyes lit up and he suddenly moved to unlock it with a wave of his hands. The magical device unclicked and allowed him to shove open the lid of the trunk. Within, several objects glowed and glimmered. Some were wrapped within protective casings, some simply gleamed with magically imbued luster. He retrieved a single oblong object.

"What's that?" Roxy asked curiously. She eagerly bounced on Immandra's lap for a look.

"If you manage to get as far as Darknoor Castle, bury this charm beneath the foundation." The dingy rag had been secured with a few pieces of twine, concealing whatever was beneath it. "Or slip it into a crack in the wall. Don't open it! It's a very powerful weapon and very destructive."

"Doesn't look like much, does it?" Kuiper murmured.

"Looks can fool you," Tarr told them wisely. "Appearances can deceive. This charm is one of the most powerful that exists. It will send a vibration through the rock. Shake the castle and bring it crashing down." A grin split his face and he chuckled. "Oh what I would give to see the expression on Thunderstone's face when it happens. Alas, I am too old for such journeys and battles."

"You aren't that old, wise Tarr. You are a very attractive man. Any lady would compete for your favors if you only gave them a chance."

Tarr glanced toward the small fox. Roxy was right. He had a handsome smile when he dared to let it show. The kind of smile that the world deserved to see more if he didn't hide it behind a dour countenance. "Why, this is the nicest thing I've heard in a long time. Do you really find me attractive?"

"Most certainly," Roxy replied.

"How would you like to stay here with me, Roxy? Keep me company."

"That is very tempting, but I'm sworn to accompany Immandra on her quest. Maybe when... it's over..." Her voice trailed and her warm eyes raised to Immandra as if seeking approval.

"You're not my pet, Roxy. You're my friend, and you're welcome to go wherever you please once we've rescued Sian."

"I shall look forward to meeting you all again. Soon, hopefully."

Immandra rose from her seat and slipped the charm into her pocket. "It's time for us to go. The sooner we're done, the sooner we can return to tell you we were successful."

"I wish you luck. Remember, many lives depend on you. More than your Sian."

Immandra couldn't thank Tarr enough. Despite their rocky start and the injuries inflicted to her borrowed body, she felt immensely relieved that their traveling party crossed his path. In the time since their overnight stay began, Tarr had also given a good brushing to Hessop's coat as well as a decent meal beneath a warm shelter. Their friend moved with renewed vigor down the road.

"What did you do that for?" Immandra asked Roxy.

"Do what?"

"Flatter that old roan so shamelessly. I think he was blushing when we left."

"Did I really? I thought I was only telling him the truth."

Kuiper huffed and turned to Immandra. "How many days left?" he asked in an abrupt change of subject. Apparently, he didn't feel comfortable discussing the handsome good looks of another man.

Immandra pulled a string from her pocket and counted a number of knots down its length. The first night after her deal with Zyda she had carefully made one-hundred knots. Every night thereafter, she untied one to keep track of their remaining time.

"Forty-six. We must hurry if we are to reach Darknoor in time, though the very thought of the place makes my skin crawl."

Roxy and Kuiper exchanged looks. Neither had the heart to tell their friend that it was likely more than the evil place causing such a sensation. Immandra looked like Zyda more and more each day. Soon there would be nothing left of Immandra.

***

Thanks to Tarr, Immandra didn't suffer so many of the negative traits of aging. An occasional sip of his rejuvenating tea eased the discomfort in her joints and gave her the willpower to carry forward. It helped to have full meals in their bellies as well.

No wonder the old man could chop wood so

impressively. He carried on like a man half his age, Immandra thought to herself. *And no wonder Roxy is so taken with him.* She'd rationed off her sips with care, wary of exhausting her supply before arriving to Darknoor. More than once, she wondered whether the war band had encountered such a difficult trail, or if the trials of her journey were exclusive to her circumstances.

"I can hardly see the path. There must be something wrong with the wand."

"Let me have a look at it," Kuiper said. His shaking of the tool didn't seem to make it operate any better. "Maybe it's out of tune or something."

"Maybe--" Hessop stumbled on the uneven ground. Startled, Immandra grasped his mane even tighter. Through luck and fortune, she remained astride the animal. "Oh no!" she cried out in concern. Without thinking of her own pains, she hastily dismounted to lead the creature by his reins.

The trail through the hills wound over rocky and treacherous ground. Dirt and loose stone shifted beneath their feet. At Kuiper's suggestion, Roxy scouted ahead, but the clever fox found no sign of easier passage.

"The sun sets early in these lands. We should make camp," Kuiper advised Immandra wisely.

"But we're running out of time."

"We'll never get anywhere if our heads are smashed against the rocks, Immandra." Roxy spoke up to her gently.

They're right... I'm so fortunate to have them with me, the young woman realized. Despite the trials of her adventure, she felt a sudden swelling of warmth and adoration for her companions. She could have never made it so far without Roxy's loving nature and Kuiper's sage advice.

They made their nightly camp with great relief. Immandra tended to Hessop first, picking chips of rock and packed dirt out of his hooves. Once she'd completed a round of care for their mount, she turned her attentions to her own needs. Her boots showed heavy signs of wear and tear. The thin soles had once been thick and tough, but now her aching feet bled.

"Forty more days..." she said, untying a knot from the length of string for the night.

"Get some sleep, Immandra. Tomorrow will be a better day," Roxy said in a worried tone. "Kuiper, come closer to the fire. You're shaking."

The cold evening air chilled them all to the bone. Their meager fire put out a pitiful amount of warmth, but it was all they had. While Roxy hunted down a couple of small pheasants to serve as their evening meal, Kuiper constructed a perfect windbreak to shelter their bodies from the harsh night air. He knotted flexible branches together as a frame, and then he packed it with fallen leaves. With the makeshift shelter to their backs, they felt only the roasting warmth of the fire against their hands and faces.

"I guess you're good for something after all," Roxy spoke up in her chipper tones.

"You both did great tonight," Immandra told them proudly. Her love for them had no boundaries, and their recent display of camaraderie had raised her spirits from their dismal point of collapse. "Thank you. I know I have not said it much, but thank you."

"Aww..." Roxy snuggled into her lap.

Kuiper sat close by to enjoy his portion of the meal provided by Roxy's hunting prowess. The little fox had outdone herself by discovering the land birds in their nest, huddled from the cold. Thanks to his ingenuitive contraption, Immandra could hardly tell that the world around them had become a snow-glazed icicle for the night.

Through teamwork, they could accomplish anything.

"Get some sleep. We'll leave at first light to make up the time."

Immandra's eyes drifted shut, only to snap open moments later. A blood-freezing howl cut through the silence of the night. Dozens more echoed after the sound.

"What... what was that?" Kuiper whispered from her lap.

"Wolfmen." Roxy peeked her nose out from Immandra's pocket. The dying firelight gleamed in her dark eyes. "They howl at the full moon, but... they may have caught our scent too."

Immandra shuddered. "I've heard terrible things about their kind."

"We should keep the fire going," Roxy warned suddenly. Her triangular ears pressed back flat against her head.

A low growl sounded from the trees. Hessop whinnied and stumbled to his feet, eyes rolling in fear. Immandra quickly grasped for his reins to keep the horned beast from fleeing.

"Too late, too late!" Roxy squealed. More snarls ripped through the air.

"Run!"

Immandra and her friends fled on foot. They left the comfort and warmth of their fire and risked the darkened trail. It was that or be eaten. Fear spurred them and terror kept their pace. Amber eyes gleamed from the trees as the wolves kept up.

"We should climb a tree!" Roxy implored.

"Hessop can't climb!"

They continued to run. Immandra held Zyda's wand out before her and prayed to every power she knew for its guidance to deliver them to safety. Their wild flight was led by the pull and tug of the wand, which took them further into rocky terrain. Their lungs burned and their breaths wheezed as they ran uphill with rocks skittering beneath their feet.

"The Blue Crescent Mountains. Perhaps we can find a cave to hide in."

"They're too close for that now." Kuiper cried.

They scrambled up the steep paths on hand and foot, pebbles and sharp stones easily abrading her palms. Roxy's tougher paw pads proved to be resistant enough that she easily moved into the lead. Kuiper's calloused digits fared well, worn from years of menial labor among his kin.

"Oh no! They'll have the scent of your blood now!" Roxy cried when she saw the bloody smears Immandra left behind. None of them dared to risk a glance over their shoulders to see the shaggy furred creatures who pursued them.

Immandra barely saw one of them out of the corner of her eye. She feared making Hessop lame on the unstable ground, but the wolves were far larger than the wild animals who dwelled in the forests surrounding Reindeer

Keep Village. A brief glance revealed feral beasts, foaming at the mouth with hunger and rage. Immandra had no desire to see them in their human guises. She imagined they would appear equally maddened.

"Are you sure this is the way?" Kuiper heavily panted in between words. It was difficult for his short legs to keep up with Immandra's longer stride. "This is barely even a trail."

"The wand says it is."

"Could the wand be lying?" Roxy yipped. The tiny fox bounded from rock to rock, trying to find them a clearer route.

"Zyda would have much to gain. She'd be able to keep your body forever," Roxy replied.

"Pray not," Immandra panted.

With the wolves hot on their tails, they had no time to worry over betrayal. It would come or it would not, but to stop and argue would mean a certain death. And a painful one.

The trail narrowed until it was little more than a track along the mountainside. They went single file, Roxy in the lead and Hessop at the rear. Immandra held tight to his reins, but gave him as much slack as she was able. She feared for his life and that the beasts would capitalize on his weakness if he fell behind.

Her fears proved to be unfounded. The noble beast harshly yanked until the reins tore free from Immandra's hold. He whirled on the trail to face their attackers as the first wolf neared. The brutal collision speared one of his golden horns through the wolf's throat and painted his ivory fur with blood.

"Hessop, no!"

"Leave! I made my promise to see you safely to Sian. I cannot keep it, but I will get you there!"

"I can't let you do this, Hessop."

"You must."

Kuiper tugged at her threadbare cloak. "Listen to him, Immandra! We have to leave or we'll all die here," the gnome protested. He urged her to continue while Roxy pleaded from her pocket. Hot tears coursed down the young girl's cheeks.

Another wolf lunged forward to the left of Hessop, snarling and snapping at Immandra's hand. She jerked back and stumbled against the rocky slope, which nearly undid her progress by sliding her downward to her doom. Hessop blocked the wolf's second attempt with his hooves, delivering a mighty storm of blows against the creature's skull. Another crept up from the side and sank its teeth into Hessop's hindquarters.

"No!" Immandra threw a rock at the snarling wolfman, but it wasn't enough. More came up the trail behind him.

They couldn't save Hessop.

Immandra grasped Kuiper's hand and ran, following Roxy. Streaks of light colored the sky, adding ribbons of gold, and rose to the dawn horizon. It was enough illumination to see the end of their path. A dead end loomed before them with a treacherous drop.

"A trap! This was all a trap!" Roxy cried.

Immandra crouched down and stared over the edge. The cliff's face was worn smooth, as if chiseled by magical fingers. There was no way to climb down. Below, a frozen river shone beneath the orange light of the rising sun.

"The only way back is full of the wolfmen." Roxy paced the edge. Her claws clicked against the thin layer of ice.

"Can't you, I don't know, talk to them?" Immandra asked.

"They won't listen to me, Kuiper. Wolves and foxes are distant cousins. Way distant."

"There's no way out," Immandra whispered. Her shoulders slumped and her graying head bowed. "We failed…"

Immandra sank down to her knees, more tired that she could possibly imagine. They had come so far, and in the end they had been led to nothing. The ground felt cold against her weathered cheek

"Sweet Mother, Lady who watches over us… If you can't save us, I beg you please grant us a painless, quick death. Do not allow my friends to suffer further." She whispered the prayer, opening tear-filled eyes to gaze upon her two friends. Kuiper and Roxy looked down at her with concerned faces.

"Jump, my child, jump. Before the creatures of darkness reach you."

Surely I am hearing things, Immandra thought. It seemed as though the very ground spoke to her. It filled her consciousness and swelled her confidence from within.

"Trust, child. Jump."

"We must jump!" she cried to Roxy and Kuiper. "Quickly, Roxy, into my pocket. I will carry you, Kuiper."

Roxy and Kuiper exchanged looks, then turned their gazes up to their friend. "We trust you."

The first wolf prowled onto the ledge. Blood glistened against his gray and black muzzle. Hessop's blood. Two other wolves of equal size came up behind the first, one gray and the other russet. All three shared the same amber shade of eyes.

Immandra looked back once, stared at their snarling faces, and promised herself she would succeed. Hessop's death would not be in vain.

She jumped.

The black wolf leapt forward and snapped. His teeth caught the end of her cloak and ripped the fabric away, but it was too late. Immandra plummeted through empty space with Kuiper tightly held in her arms.

Thin icy surface of the river parted before Immandra's disbelieving eyes. The black waters beneath rose in rippling waves of current, and the three plunged into its chilly embrace. The cold stole her breath away. It sent lances of pain through her body and burned her skin. Shocked, she instinctively gasped for a breath.

Chapter Nine

A Friend

Kuiper struggled free from Immandra's weakening hold, feeling lost in the dark and chilling water. He grabbed at her ragged clothes, tugging and pulling in a futile attempt to bring his drowning friend to the surface. Dark shapes converged on them, bringing further panic to the struggling gnome. The sleek bodies came into view, three river otters nearly twice Kuiper's size. They placed themselves beneath Immandra's arms and brought the whole group up into the fresh air.

Kuiper gasped, wheezing air into his burning lungs. "Thank the Mother! Thank you!"

The otters ferried them to the shore and dragged them all up over the ice encrusted grass. Kuiper worriedly checked on Immandra, relief flooding his little body when she saw that she breathed. Her skin was pale, her lips blue, but Immandra was alive.

"Roxy!"

Hurriedly he fished the little fox out of Immandra's

pocket. Roxy looked tiny, her fur soaked through and flat instead of bushy and fluffed out. She sneezed and panted, trembling in his hold.

"I must get them shelter," Kuiper cried, looking to the otters. "Please, we will all freeze out here in the wind's bitter bite."

The otters chittered and squeaked, then they began pulling Immandra by her clothes further up the shore. Kuiper followed and helped. They brought him to a hollow in the hill, only a few feet deep, but wide and tall enough for their needs. They dragged Immandra within and Kuiper raggedly thanks the otters again, praising them for the rescue. Then he set about making a fire while Roxy snuggled in beneath Immandra's chin.

"Will she be alright?"

"I hope so," Kuiper whispered. "Here, this fire should warm us all up some."

"I'm so cold," Roxy whined pitifully.

"I'll go catch us some fish to make a stew--" Kuiper began, only to fall silent when the otters returned. They each dropped a large, wriggling fish down at the entrance. Tears glistened in the gnome's eyes. "Thank you again, kind friends."

Soon he had their small pot over the fire, the fish chopped up and cooking inside. Roxy had taken her small portion raw to ease the ache in her belly, but she sniffed appreciatively at the pot.

"It's lucky we are that Tarr provided such an enchanted bag. Not a thing within lost or ruined," Roxy said. They had discovered the miraculous sight when preparing the meal. Immandra lay covered in a dry blanket which seemed to have eased her quaking limbs.

For the second time since their departure from the wizard's home, Tarr's magic had come in handy and saved them.

"R- Roxy? Kuiper?"

Immandra's voice startled them both and they gleefully cried out when they saw her opened eyes.

"Shush now, Immandra. Eat. Warm yourself first, then we can talk." Kuiper dished up bowls of hot stew for everyone.

"You're not a bad cook," Roxy commented. She lapped the broth of Kuiper's fish stew from the wooden bowl.

"Thank you. I thought I wouldn't live long enough to hear a compliment from your lips," Kuiper quipped.

"I could use a little more," Immandra murmured. She glumly sat beside the fire with the blanket around her shoulders. She couldn't get her mind off of Hessop and his last stand. He'd given his life for her, and now she had nothing of him left but his memory. "I thought that was going to be the end of us."

"Poor Hessop," Roxy said. The fox shook her head and mournfully pushed away her bowl with a paw.

"Hessop knew what he was doing, Immandra. He saved all of us."

"I know… I only wish that he was with us. We'll always cherish him in our memories," Immandra decided. When Kuiper sneezed and began to cough into one of his small fists, she quickly refilled his bowl. "Have some more of your own medicine."

"I guess his strange devotion to fishing finally proved useful," Roxy commented. "The stew is excellent."

"I'll go rinse the pot, so as not to attract further predators. You two warm yourselves." Immandra rose shakily.

"No, no, you should stay. I can do it," Kuiper argued.

Immandra leaned down and kissed his head gently. "You have done more than enough. Let me help you this time. Stay with Roxy."

She trekked down to the river and knelt. First things first, she rinsed their cooking pot and bowls as promised. Only a thin, oily film had remained of their meal. Every bite had been eaten.

"Wise Waters, thank you for sending your children to our aid. Now I must call upon your help again," Immandra said quietly. She looked down at her reflection in the slushy surface. "I must find Sian, my soulmate. If I do not reach Darknoor, all will be lost."

"It is you again," the waters sighed. "We showed you all we knew. Go ask elsewhere."

"There is no one else to ask," Immandra pleaded. "Please, I trust in your wisdom. Please try again."

"Persistent, you are. Fine then. Look upon the water, child, and concentrate. Focus on what you wish to know and see."

Immandra reached down and broke up the slurry of ice, creating a cleared area of dark water. She clasped her hands to her breast and looked down, focusing all her thoughts on her husband. The waters wavered and darkened, then an image began to bloom across the surface. Matta Dora's face shimmered before her vision, sparking Immandra's recognition. The acrimonious expression, overflowing with contempt, shrank Immandra back in terror. Someone's actions infuriated the Princess of Darkness, and contorted her features into a hate-filled mask. Behind the woman's image, Immandra recognized three figures - Giber, Yorteze, and Sian. All three were chained to the wall.

"What do you wish, Zyda? That is you, is it not? You look terrible, you old hag. I promised myself I would kill you next time we met."

Immandra gasped. She wasn't seeing an image of a memory or a distant view. Somehow she had reached through to Matta herself. The princess' voice was razor sharp, cold as the blackest ice.

"I am not Zyda. I am Immandra Stillwater of Sinead. You hold my friends prisoner. You hold my soulmate."

"Which one? This one?" Matta jabbed a finger towards Yorteze. The proud sylvan looked broken and weathered. "You make a nice couple, the hag and the rotting tree. To set your heart at ease, I will kill him before your eyes."

"Yorteze is not my soulmate. Sian is."

Matta laughed. "Surely you joke. You? You look more to be his grandmother."

"I am his wife."

Matta crossed to the wall and grabbed Sian's chin in her hand. His eyes rolled back in his head. "I am rather fond of this one. I will make him my pet. My lover."

"Oh no you won't!" Immandra cried. "He wouldn't want you anyways. Your heart is black as pitch."

"Tsk tsk," Matta chided. "You underestimate my powers. I can easily make him love me. Serve me. Do whatever I desire. A single spell is all it takes."

"Don't you dare! I'll kill you--"

Cruel laughter spilled from Matta Dora's lips. "Kill

me? You? You are but a fool, Immandra Stillwater of Sinead. An old hag with no powers at your call." Matta stretched out her clawed hand and quickly began to murmur an incantation.

Immandra drew back, startled, and her foot knocked a loose bit of rock into the water. The image vanished with the first ripple and splash.

"Sian…"

"We'll get to him."

Immandra quickly turned and discovered Kuiper and Roxy both standing a few feet away. They came to her side and embraced her as she dropped to her knees with tears dripping down her cheeks. Even now her friends brought her comfort and strength. She would need both.

***

The sounds of merriment escaped the tavern each time an approaching traveler entered its doors. Immandra and her friends hurried across the filthy layer of snow leading up to the inn. Two days had passed since losing Hessop and their hearts were all the more heavy for his loss. Nothing could replace him, but they longed for another mount to lighten the burden of their travels.

Immandra's belly rumbled with hunger for a complete meal that didn't consist of dried rations or fish. Kuiper was able to supply them with sustenance easily enough, but she wanted to enjoy something that didn't come from a body of water. Kuiper and Roxy practically raced one another up the creaky wooden steps, eager to enter the warm environment of the bar.

"Be careful, Imma. The steps are slick," Roxy called

back in warning. She anxiously bounced up and down by the tavern's entrance.

"There may be robbers, thieves, and highway bandits in a place like this. *I* personally don't mind, but this is no place for a lady. I'll have to protect you both," Kuiper declared.

Roxy giggled. Kuiper's courageous words even brought a smile to Immandra's tired face. For the first time in days, she laughed. She truly did resemble Zyda when she entered the inn and fell under scrutiny of the tall, gaunt man behind the bar. The fellow's single beady eye followed her movements, but seemed to ignore the petite fox and small gnome traveling underfoot.

The scent of roasting meats and baked goods filled Immandra's nose. A thick and hearty stew boiled and bubbled in the tavern's kitchen area. Nearby, a cloaked man bit into flaky biscuits and mopped up the brown broth remaining in the bowl. Kuiper's belly noisily rumbled as they passed the solitary diner. He wore his hood while eating, so most of his features were concealed. Immandra saw only a smooth lower face and his sleek black hair spilling out from the dark hood.

A gang of ruffians occupied another table in the tavern's darkest corner where the light from the hearth failed to penetrate the shadows. They guzzled ales and uttered crude words to the serving wench.

"Rude!" Roxy cried indignantly.

The burliest and largest of the men groped the passing bar wench. His hand practically covered the poor woman's entire rump. She swatted him and uttered words of protest that the group drowned out with their boisterous laughter.

Nothing about their behavior seemed funny to Immandra. "Agreed," she said.

Upset by the manhandling, the bar wench stormed into the rear of the tavern to disappear beyond a door. Immandra couldn't blame her. She'd be upset too if some thug had taken liberty with grabbing her so brazenly. Not that anyone would while she resembled Zyda. The man was clearly too self-absorbed to realize he'd truly upset the woman. Many of the other tavern occupants seemed equally disturbed. The one-eyed bartender kept a close watch, but said nothing.

"Should we say something?" Kuiper asked.

"Say something, Imma!" Roxy entreated her.

Immandra sighed. If no one else would speak out about their crude behavior, then she would have to do it. She cleared her throat first. "Hasn't your mother taught you anything about how to treat a woman?" she demanded in a loud voice.

The merry-making and jesting quieted briefly. Several eyes turned her way. The leader, a broad-shouldered man with a mane of ebon hair, boldly laughed and shook his head. "Jealous, you old hag? You're probably just mad that no one makes a pass at you these days."

It hurt. It stung as acutely as any other insult, but she consoled herself with thoughts of Sian and how much he loved her. Zyda's body wasn't her true form and the wretched appearance was only a temporary measure. One she had to use to her advantage somehow.

"If she didn't want the kind of attention we gave her, she wouldn't come out dressed like a whore," another man spoke up. "Ain't that right, Beeron?"

"Too right, my friend. That wench got what she was asking for," Beeron said. He chuckled and swigged from his ale. He wiped his mouth with the back of his hand and focused his gaze on Immandra. He had enough brawn to break her in half if he wanted to.

"No! No one deserves to be touched and groped without their permission."

"What are you going to do about it, hag?"

The other men at the table quieted, seeming reluctant to speak up. There were tales and stories of terrifying witches, such as Zyda and Matta, of course, and they easily circulated around the world of Sinead through word of mouth.

Fine. If I've got her body, then I need to play the part. They'll never learn otherwise, Immandra decided. "I'll turn you into a frog!" she threatened.

The laughter ceased immediately. The same uneasy whispers traveled through the small group. She strained to listen and picked up the word 'Bitternel' among the hushed sounds.

That's right. Believe I'm Zyda this time. If it will teach you manners. Immandra quickly glanced at Roxy and Kuiper to see that both were attempting to hide behind her. "If you doubt me, ask her!" she said as she swept aside by a step to reveal Roxy. "Tell them of the price you paid for defying me, Roxy."

Kuiper snickered behind her tattered skirts, but Roxy could have been a stage actress for a play. She fell into her part easily. "I was once her servant, but she did this to me! I may never get my human body back again," the fox cried.

"See, it's true! She really is Zyda Bitternel, mistress of the changing shape! Beeron, if you upset her, you might end up worse than a frog. Maybe a fly," another of his drinking pals warned him.

The rowdy group and their leader remained very silent. They dropped a pile of silver on their table and left disgruntled to their rooms. Immandra sighed in relief and gingerly lowered to her seat. The days spent in the unrelenting cold hadn't helped her aging bones, and she looked forward to a night in an actual bed. Since leaving Tarr's residence, she'd eagerly looked forward to returning to Reindeer Keep Village with Sian. She also looked forward to their friends, their new home, and a life together as husband and wife.

Immandra didn't realize that she'd drifted into a daze until Roxy pawed her leg.

"Imma! Tell her what you want," Roxy said.

Immandra snapped out of it to see the same bar wench standing beside their table. Kuiper had already taken a seat in one of the chairs, even if his face barely came up to the table. Roxy scrambled onto a chair and leapt onto the table opposite them.

"Thanks for that. For chasing off those men. They've been harassing us all day, but Calden's too scared they'll pick a big fight in the bar."

"You're welcome." She wasn't behaving very much like Zyda, but that didn't really matter now. Her little act had been enough to chase off the threat.

Kuiper lacked the imagination to order anything but baked fish. Roxy and Immandra snickered and ordered servings of mutton stew. They eagerly buttered the rolls of thick bread brought in a basket to their table.

The starving trio dined as if they'd never seen a meal in all of their lives.

They ate away the pain of losing Hessop, the despair produced by the inevitable confrontation with Matta Dora, and the fear of losing Immandra's true form forever. Stuffing their faces in silence, neither of them heard the subtle scuff of a chair against the wooden floor, or heard approaching boot steps, until the cloaked stranger arrived just behind Immandra. If her old bones weren't practically crumbling, she would have leapt from her chair in fright.

"A fine performance. Had I not known better, I may have been fooled. For a moment."

"What performance?" Immandra asked. Uneasiness straightened her crooked spine, at least, it partially straightened the curve to her back. She set a distrustful gaze upon the hooded man.

An iron key clicked against the table, placed by a pale golden hand. Slender, articulate fingers pushed it forward. "Top floor, last door on the left. Sleep would suit you well after such a harrowing journey. Worry no further of my intentions, I do not come to trouble you. I bring words of guidance."

"You can't go to a strange room with a strange man, Imma," Kuiper whispered.

"He's hardly stranger than you," Roxy stated primly. The fox delicately sniffed the unknown man's wrist, which bravely lingered within reach for that very purpose. Satisfied with whatever she smelled, Roxy then touched her cheek against his hand. He obliged her with a scratch against her furry face that eventually reached her small chin.

"She has a point," Immandra said. She ignored the sour face from Kuiper. "We'll meet with you then."

"Do not tary long. You frightened the ruffians away, but worse travel this road." With his final words, the cloaked man turned and left, disappearing through the door to outside. If he meant to join them upstairs, he was coming by a different way.

"Maybe he's waiting till we fall asleep and will murder us in our beds."

"He wouldn't have spent the coin on a room for that. Besides, he smells trustworthy. Like a friend. Familiar even," Roxy mused.

They finished their meals in silence, but when the time came to pay for their food, the bartender and his wench waved them off. It was on the house. Immandra didn't argue it. She graciously accepted the gift with a smile, although her face had aged so greatly that the sagging flesh made her features resemble more of a grimace. That too, helped her to fall into the role of pretending to be Zyda.

"You shouldn't smile anymore," Roxy said. "Or try to anyway. I think you scared them."

"Thanks, Roxy." Immandra sighed and continued up the steps with the aid of the cane.

Roxy fell back a few paces, her bright eyes large and wide in her tiny face. "I'm sorry!" she cried. Recently, more and more, her open and mouthy little friend had begun to recognize the harm in her disparaging comments.

"It's alright.

They found their new acquaintance seated in a creaky old chair beside a small round table. A single lantern glowed upon it, casting its yellow radiance over the tiny room.

"At last. I began to fear you would simply leave without allowing me this chance to speak with you in private. Please, close the door. The spies of the enemy lurk in distant places such as this."

Kuiper nudged the door shut, but then Roxy race up his short body to stand upon his back and shoulders, earning a cry of disapproval from the small gnome. She turned the lock with her teeth and scampered down.

"Enemy? Spies?"

"Of course. Just as your village and the Mountain Fliers have sent a scouting party to investigate the occurrences in Darknoor, so has Matta Dora employed the use of spies to infiltrate these distant villages." He swept his hood away from his face, displaying handsome features and fair skin.

Hair, black as a raven's wing, fell around the man's face and past his shoulders. Pointed ears peeked out of the silken strands at an elegant angle, revealing his fairy heritage. His charming smile set her worries to rest near instantly.

"You're a fairy," Immandra said, awed. A flush crept up her decrepit cheeks, realizing she'd merely stated the obvious.

"Astute observation, dear Immandra. I am. I come to bring a warning of the trials ahead, for you will face many of them in the coming days."

Had she not already endured many dangers on the path to Darknoor? Where were the fairies then when she'd needed their help. Immandra licked her dry, wrinkled lips and wished for a glass of water. Anticipating her need for a drink, the fairy offered her an ornate wine skin. Warm liquid flowed over her tongue, its sweet flavor derived from the berries of Sibba's personal garden.

"Do you like it?"

"Yes, thank you," she said, handing the bag back.

Roxy and Kuiper took seats on the bed, glad to be off their feet and to be warm. The man smiled at them both then waved his hand in their direction. Roxy yawned and Kuiper fell flat to his back atop the blankets.

"What--"

"Worry not for your friends, they are merely asleep. What I have to say is for your ears alone, but I would not have denied them the comforts of the room."

Immandra checked on both her friends, but as promised, they were alive and well. Roxy lay curled against Kuiper's side and both appeared relaxed and content.

"Alright then." She remained on her feet, still distrustful of his motives. "Why are you here now? I thought Lady Sibba did all that she could for me."

"She has, and she hasn't," the mysterious fairy said to her. "I am Ordalf, a humble knight of the lady. I have come not at her behest, but to fulfill my own selfish interests."

"Your own? This has nothing to do with Matta Dora?"

"It does and it doesn't," he answered. His cryptic choice of words ran a chill over her limbs. He rose from the seat to approach her, "I have often watched you, Immandra of the Lindens. Immandra the fair and bright, with fire in her hair." His fingers stroked down her lank and dry hair. For a moment, Immandra saw her natural auburn hue beneath the ashy gray, but only for a blink of an eye.

Only my imagination. My hair is dry as straw and dull as stone. "Why would you watch me?" she voiced out loud.

"Would you not like to end this miserable journey?" he countered. He didn't answer her question. Although the surroundings were warmed by the venting chambers, a cold sensation numbed her fingers and toes.

"Of course I want it to end," Immandra said quietly, hands fisting at her sides. "I want to bring my husband home. My friends. I want the snows to go away before my people starve."

"They are humans. Nothing more. They multiply like rodents, clearing away our beautiful forests."

Immandra opened her mouth, but no words came out. Anger surged, bringing tension to her crooked spine. She barely resisted spewing hateful words at the man.

"And so, we have devised a plan to deal with Matta Dora. We will allow her to reap her devastation for now. As the winters end and spring returns, the fae will once more reach the height of our power. We will destroy her then, but not a day sooner."

"That's horrible!" she cried. "How could the fairies even consider such a thing?"

"We have long grown tired of the infestation known as humanity. They crawl far and wide, clearing away our beautiful forests, spreading sickness wherever they travel. A plague."

"That isn't true. Sibba loves humans. She came to my wedding. She gifted me and Sian with *these* rings," Immandra insisted, thrusting her left hand in the handsome fairy's face. She showed him her enchanted ring, but a slow smile spread over his face.

"Come away with me now and end this foolish journey. I will restore your body and your true form. You belong in the land of your mother, dearest Immandra. Alongside me, you will become a princess among our people, for Lady Sibba has no legitimate heirs and has chosen her loyal knight as her successor. I need only the proper bride to sit the throne alongside me. I have chosen you."

"But… I am wed to Sian. I love him."

"Did not Matta Dora say to you that she would take him as her lover? He is lost, Immandra. Caught in her magic from which there is no return, save death. Let me spare you that pain."

"How could you even know that?" Wariness led her to take a small step backwards.

Ordalf pulled an ornate mirror from his cloak. Its polished silver face shimmered with iridescent hues. "I have watched your path. It was I who whispered to the otters of your need. I who coaxed the breezes to carry your song. I wanted to come to you then, but I knew your travels would bring you here to me. So I waited."

The mirror cast a reflection of Immandra's restored youth, bright eyes no longer dulled by age and cataracts. Her sleek hair pooled over her shoulders bared by an exquisite summer gown.

Live among the fairies. My night there was wondrous… How it must be to live with them always, dancing and singing beneath the crystals of the earth… The daydream flitted through her mind, vivid and strong. She waltzed on Ordalf's arm, dressed in airy silks with jewels shining on her brow. She was without fears and worries. And she was without sadness. Merriment and joy rang from every corner of the room.

Immandra wanted it. She wanted to shed Zyda's body and have her own returned. To be happy again.

"No..." *No, how can I ever be happy without Sian? Without Druid Thorn's guidance and Giber's laughter. Even Dool's sour nature has its place in our village. He acts stern, but he never fails to lend a hand.* "No," she repeated. Ordalf's mouth turned down at the corners, his mood dimmed by her resolute tone.

"Surely you cannot mean that."

Immandra lifted her chin a fraction. "I do. I cannot give up now, not when I have come so far and am so close to rescuing them."

"How will you save them? You travel by foot with no food, heading into the unknown with a wizard's toy as your only tool."

"We came this far," she continued stubbornly. "We'll find a way to make the last leg of the journey. I won't give up on Sian. I'll save my people and the rest of our human villages with or without help from the fairies."

A slow smile spread over Ordalf's face. "Then I must congratulate you, Immandra Stillwater. You have passed the final test." He bowed deeply to her, conveying his respect.

"I-- You--" Immandra wasn't sure whether to be angry, confused, or relieved. A frown furrowed her brow.

"I apologize for my dishonesty, but I could not grant my aid without knowing your true heart. Indeed, I am disappointed a life as pure as your own belongs to another man, but I will not abandon you."

"I love Sian. Lady Sibba herself blessed our marriage." Immandra lightly perched on the foot of the bed. "What help will the fairies offer?"

"The words of our Queen remain true. We cannot help, for this is not our season. We will not return to power until the height of spring, and by then, Matta Dora will have become the destruction of humans and sylvan alike. We are all doomed, and yet our Queen remains reluctant to give her aid for other reasons which are our own."

"Then what is it you mean to do?"

"For tonight, you have hot food in your bellies and a warm, clean bed. When dawn breaks you will have another filling meal. Darknoor lies only a few hours walk from this place by this winding trail."

Ordalf offered a map. It pictured the Inn, the forest, the main roads, and Darknoor. The fairy pointed to a line of green ink drawn through the forest.

"A shortcut known to very few. Once, when this land was a brighter place, our rangers used this as a hunting trail. Keep the stone markers to your left and the wooden to your right, and you will find your way."

"Thank you."

"I have one last gift, Immandra." He stepped close and drew a fine golden chain from his pocket. He wound it round and round her wrist three times, then clasped the delicate piece of jewelry. "May this protect you from Matta Dora's vile magic. Light to cancel the darkness. I cannot remain here any longer to protect you."

"Ordalf?" she called after he stepped away towards the door.

Ordalf drew his hood up over his head of lustrous

black hair and lingered at the door. He glanced back at her over one shoulder. "Yes?"

"What would you have done if I had chosen your offer?"

"Why, my dear, I would have swept you away into a life beyond your fantasy. And we fairies would have hunkered down for a long winter's rest."

Once Ordalf departed the room and shut the door behind him, Immandra secured it against unwanted intrusion and settled into the bed. The thin blankets provided only enough warm that she didn't shiver as she fell into her easy sleep.

In her dreams, Reindeer Keep Village flourished beneath the warmth of the summer sun as she danced around the bonfire alongside her beloved.

***

A wide plain spread out before them, dotted with stone statues. The blackened walls of Darknoor rose up above them, and beyond the castle, and soared like a jagged spear towards the sky. Its presence cast a malignant shadow.

Immandra heavily leaned on her staff and stared. Her dark blue eyes filled with trepidation. Beside her, Kuiper and Roxy tensely waited, neither brave enough to venture forward alone.

"Those statues, they look like people. What gruesome sculptures," the gnome uttered tersely. His fingers squeezed over the hilt of his cudgel.

"They're creepy. I don't like them," Roxy added.

"These are the people and beings who have offended

the Masters of Darknoor," Immandra whispered. "They turned them to stone. My mother once told me of it in a story. And the number of ornaments only grows with each failed assault on her castle."

Kuiper restlessly shifted on his feet. "Risky business, messing with these two. Can they only turn one into stone, or other things?"

"Let's pray we don't find out." Roxy swished her tail. The small fox took the first tentative steps forward. "Come on then, we may as well get across while we have the light. The sun will set soon."

The first statue they passed resembled a boy of nearly adult years. Immandra slowed to study his face, and shook her head. "So very young. Barely a grown man."

"Is there anything we can do?" Kuiper asked. He hurried over to another statue, recognizing two of his gnomish kin clinging together. Their terror was forever frozen on their faces.

"Only the death of Matta Dora and Mizar Thunderstone could free them."

"You mean, all these people would come to life again?"

"So say the stories," Immandra replied to Roxy.

"Someone needs to get serious about that." Kuiper poked at the stone gnomes.

"Many tried. Sian and the others tried. And now… now *we* are trying. And we can't fail."

The trio trudged forward, intent on making their destination. The sun mercilessly burned overhead and their every footstep stirred up a cloud of dust. No snow marred the ground here. No ice spread. Yet the air was bitter cold, even beneath the sun's rays.

"Do you ever wonder where they came from?" Roxy asked.

"Matta Dora claimed the fortress from a countess who once ruled this land," Immandra answered her.

"No. Who is she? Where did she come from? She had a mother at some point, didn't she?"

"I'm sure her mother is very ashamed of her right now," Kuiper said.

Immandra weakly chuckled at her friends. Despite the serious nature of their discussion, their idle chatter was a needed reprieve from the dismal fate awaiting them.

Night swiftly fell, and the temperatures plummeted with it. Overhead, the full moon shone with a clear and cold light.

"Should we stop? There are some rocks here at least we can shelter behind. That castle must be huge, it seems we have barely travelled any closer to it."

Immandra shook her head. "No, Kuiper. I'd like to cover as much distance as we can. This close, I feel as if I could walk all night and day without a single stop."

"I have always been fond of moonlit walks," Kuiper mused in an effort to keep spirits up. "Romantic."

"You've never struck me as the romantic sort, Kuiper," Roxy snorted. Immandra looked down at them both with an amused smile.

Her two friends bantered and Immandra contented herself to listen. It was good to hear them playfully tease one another instead of trading mean-spirited jabs. It lightened the somber mood that weighed on her shoulders. Instead of dreading her arrival to Darknoor, she allowed her mind to wander to the future. She imagined a future with Sian in their humble cottage. She dreamed of children with his fair eyes and her dark copper hair. A smile contorted the wrinkled lips of Immandra's aged mouth as the whimsical vision danced through her mind. It helped give her more strength to carry on.

"Kuiper! See that movement in the sky?"

Roxy's sudden cry drew Immandra out of her daydreaming. "What is it?" she asked.

"Looks like huge birds circling around the castle. What are they?" Kuiper asked.

"Doom Fliers, most likely," Roxy replied.

Most people across the lands had heard some tale or another about the fabled Doom Fliers of Darknoor. Kuiper shuddered. "They're more terrifying than I imagined. They give me the creeps," he said.

"And with good reason. They are awful creatures, something between a human and a scavenger bird. They can be manipulated by whoever they are keyed to."

"Are they magical?" Immandra asked.

"Yes. They have little intelligence of their own, but in the hands of an expert magician, they turn into a powerful weapon."

"Does that mean that someone in the castle is controlling them and looking through their eyes?" Kuiper asked. Gnomes were also known for their own ingenuity and natural proclivity for technological tools. But they never would have conceived something as wicked as controlling another creature by magic like a living puppet. "How do you know so much, Roxy?"

Yes, how indeed, Immandra wondered.

"I may have listened in while Chappeewa spoke

with Druid Thorn," Roxy admitted. "After all, their Mountain Fliers are the ones Matta takes and twists to her whims. He said it is worse than death, what their once loyal mounts suffer."

"Just another reason for us to bring Darknoor down."

Immandra and Kuiper crouched down behind one of the stone figures to watch the winged monstrosities. The fliers soared high above them on the frigid winds. Their eyes glowed like red stars against the sky.

"If they detect us, they'll tear us to pieces," Kuiper said.

Kuiper jinxed them. One of the fliers suddenly banked left and veered back toward the group.

"We were spotted!" Roxy cried, dismayed.

"Run for cover," Immandra shouted.

They ran for a formation of nearby rocks, but it could do little good against the creatures who would only land on the ground to hunt them out. She feared the bite of their beaks and their sharp talons. Unlike the brigands in the tavern, the Doom Fliers wouldn't be diverted by the threat of magic she didn't have.

Immandra and Kuiper crawled between the boulders. Roxy had an easier time of digging beneath the dust and dry dirt sheltered from the snow. Her smaller body easily became hidden from sight. A blanket of dust concealed her completely. Kuiper was another issue altogether. He found a crack in the rocks, but his gnome-sized body couldn't fit. His bottom stuck out for all to see.

Roxy stuck out her head from her hideaway, but she coughed on the dust and dirt clouding her vision. "That's not good enough! We need help. The ring… maybe the wand too. Imma, try something!"

The Doom Fliers continued on their fast course. They swooped down with their talons bared. Their enormous, tooth-filled beaks seemed razor sharp in the pale moonlight.

Immandra and her friends were going to die.

***

Matta Dora chuckled over the view of her castle's barren plains. She enjoyed the sight of her handiwork, but took even more pleasure in the feeling of immense power. Soon, all of Sinead would know her wrath. They would bow before her might and happily accept her rule.

At a table nearby, Mizar and General Stern continued a game of Chess. She ignored them in favor of enjoying the landscape through the eyes of her pets. She had no doubt that soon someone would arrive in pursuit of her newest acquisitions. Where there were few, more were bound to come.

Let them come, she thought. Happily cackling, she prepared to pull free from the view of her flying pets. Just as she began to close the psychic link between her mind's eye and the sight of the Doom Fliers, she saw two shapes traveling the plain. *Fine. Let them come. The more the merrier. My dungeon hungers for new flesh, my bowl for more blood.* She sent the Fliers winging closer to their prey, only to recognize the weathered features of the old hag in the lead. Her excited squeal drew Mizar's attention away from the game.

"What is it, my dear Matta?"

"It's her! It's Zyda Bitternel!"

"Our old friend, Zyda? Well, well, well. To come near our castle... she has guts." Mizar took the helm of the viewing glass and gazed through the Fliers' eyes. "They are nearly here."

"Good. Let them come. Our soldiers will be ready," General Stern spoke out loud. His voice loudly rumbled, resonating with power. It was a power Zyda would soon feel once his army was unleashed. "Shall we destroy her now, my Queen?"

"No," Matta Dora murmured. "No. You must let her come to me. I have longed for the opportunity to dispense justice to Zyda Bitternell in my own special way. I wish to grant death to her myself."

"As you wish," the General bowed.

"Now leave me, both of you. But send me my chosen pet, Mizar. I think it is time I broke him..."

"Now?"

Matta grinned. "Oh yes. Zyda claims him as her own. I will make him mine."

Mizar and the General left her chambers, leaving Matta to prepare. She set her magical tools aside and changed her clothes, eagerly anticipating her next move.

She slowly paced the length of her lavish room, thoughts full of wicked and delightful revenge. Her robe whispered against the floor with every step, the crimson fabric barely concealing the black lace worn beneath. The negligee showed off the perfection of her curvaceous body and the flawless canvas of her pale skin.

"Enter," she called at the sound of a knock upon the door. Two guards stepped inside, leading Sian between them. With a wave from her hand, she dismissed the pair, then she circled her prisoner.

Sian stood tall with as much pride as he could muster. His wet hair shined dark gold beneath the lantern light and his new shirt damply clung to his body. Matta had ordered him to be bathed. She had no doubts the experience had been unpleasant for him, but the end result was all that mattered. He was clean. The stench of her dungeon and his weeks of imprisonment no longer clung to him.

"Such a handsome man," Matta crooned, coming to stand before him. "A face as pretty as yours can take you far in life."

Sian sneered, his revulsion plainly written across his strong features. "What do you want from me?"

"Guess..." Matta grinned and traced a hand across her collarbone.

"Never," Sian declared. "I love only one woman, my wife. My soulmate. My Immandra. You are not she nor can you ever be."

"Immandra..." Matta stepped closer, brushing up against Sian lightly. The way he tensed brought her no end of pleasure. "Immandra... now where have I heard that name? No matter. I can persuade you to forget all about her. To charge the object of your adoration."

"She is my only love," he repeated firmly.

Matta leaned in close until her nose brushed against his, her words low and soft, "Don't be so sure about that, Sian."

A swift turn took her away from the man. She crossed to her dresser then pulled out a single jar from the top drawer. She withdrew a single pinchful of sparkling rose colored dust, then crossed back. She blew the shimmering powder into Sian's face and whispered quietly. Sian struggled against the bonds of her magic, but it was a futile attempt. The determination and outrage faded from his features. For a moment, he looked confused and lost. Matta waited the space of a breath then lifted her magical restraints. Sian's face turned to hers and his eyes widened.

"My lady..." Sian sunk to his knees before her, a dreamy smile on his face. He leaned in and pressed his lips to her belly.

Matta smiled and ran her fingers through his drying her. "See? I told you I can change things around here..."

"Yes, my lady. My love..."

***

"Imma, hurry!" Roxy urged her.

Immandra concentrated on the ring with all of her willpower. Nothing changed. "Mother, help us! Just one time more!"

A warm, familiar voice spoke up. It was heartfelt and genuine, soothing to her senses during a time of anxiety and fear. "Look into your heart, child. I can do nothing when it's filled with shadows."

Immandra forced herself to draw in several calming and deep breaths. *I have to do this. I have to clear the darkness from my heart, or we'll all die.* She relaxed her haggard features and let thoughts of benevolence come to mind. She thought of her love Sian, her desire to protect Roxy and Kuiper, and her longing for Hessop to not have died in vain. Hessop had paid an incredible price for them to come so far.

The Doom Fliers screamed as they fell in an amazing descent. Saliva glistened upon their needlelike teeth. At that very moment, the ground stirred beneath Immandra. She felt it moving under her feet, and a shudder ran through the rocks. Four strange configurations pushed from the soil and arched above their heads, growing toward one another until they met in the middle. It formed a small cave illuminated by coin-sized quartz stones. Each one glowed like a tiny star.

From within their shelter, they heard the Doom Fliers landing against the mound of stone. They screeched in frustration and scratched at the ground with their clawed feet, but their talons failed to dislodge the rocks. It was sealed tight. The avian creatures continued to scream and struggle for a while longer until only the sound of their steps remained.

"That was a s-s-surprising t-t-turn of events," Kuiper stammered.

"Relax, friend. It's over now," Roxy told him.

"Wait until daylight, my children. Doom Fliers are creatures of the night. They will leave by dawn to return to their wicked masters," the earth said.

"Thank you," Immandra whispered venerably. Kuiper and Roxy echoed her words of gratitude.

The voice faded but left a gentle feeling of encouraging warmth that didn't fade for some time. Unable to sleep and find good rest, Immandra and her friends discussed their plans for reaching the castle.

"I'm not sure if I can face Sian looking like this."

"Don't tell him it's you. Tell him Immandra sent you," Roxy suggested.

"I can't lie to Sian. I have to tell him the truth."

"Let's hope that he is a very understanding man, and that he loves you enough to overlook certain details," Roxy said uncertainly.

"He'd better be after all Immandra's gone through for him."

"Males can't be trusted. As long as you're young and beautiful maybe, but after that... well. I don't know Sian as well as I know you, Imma. I only hope that what we're doing for him is worth it."

Immandra rarely heard such words of wisdom from her fox friend. She held as tightly to her faith as she could. Her heart had to remain filled with truth, warmth, and light. As soon as she gave into darkness, she would lose the fight. "Don't say that, Roxy. There are bonds stronger than that in this world."

"I've never experienced anything like that in my life," Roxy said.

"What about Tarr? You're a fox and he offered to let you stay with him. You liked him for how he was without caring about his looks."

Roxy quieted and ducked her head.

"Tomorrow will be a difficult day. I'll need your help."

"You can count on us," Kuiper assured Immandra. He lightly kicked Roxy with the toe of his foot

"He's right. We're here for you. Sian will see you for who you are, Immandra. Trust in that."

The three friends moved closer and held one another close. They listened to the sounds of searching Doom Fliers until exhaustion and sweet oblivion finally claimed them.

Hours later, sunlight filtered in through the narrow cracks of their stone shelter and awakened the small group. Roxy stretched and Immandra yawned, while Kuiper sleepily mumbled about fish. The gnome startled awake when Roxy licked his nose. "Ah!"

"C'mon sleepyhead, day is upon us."

"Our last day…" Immandra held out her length of string. A single knot remained.

"Well, uh, how do we get out of here? There's no door." Kuiper looked around their safe haven.

"A moment." Immandra held her ring over her heart. "Thank you for helping us, Mother. It is time we finish our quest, but you have left us no door…"

No voice reached out to them, but the stones began to shudder. Bits of dust drifted down over them, then the rocks sank back into the ground where they had come from. After the deep darkness, the morning light was almost blinding.

"Look, we're closer than I'd thought," Roxy said excitedly.

With the end in sight, they moved with renewed purpose. An hour's walk brought them to the imposing gate. They crossed the drawbridge over a moat. The water looked thick and murky, with bubbles popping across its viscous surface. Immandra didn't dare to wonder what caused it.

"Guards!" Roxy hissed softly. "Wolfmen by the looks and smell of it."

Two armored men stood at the far end of the bridge. Their hair shaggily hung around their furred faces. Claws tipped their ungloved hands and looked as sharp as the spears they held.

"Halt! Where do you think you're going, old hag?" the first guard asked. When he spoke it showed his sharp, yellowed canines.

"Er... I am only off to the markets. I want to trade my gnome for herbs and spices from far kingdoms. Surely you have a market here."

The two guards exchanged glances. "We are under strict orders. All who seek to enter the castle are to be brought to the Princess of Darkness. You will come with us."

"I'll just come to market some other time then..." Immandra took a hesitant step backwards. She turned away, but strong hands grabbed her from either side.

"You heard us, hag. You're not going anywhere."

Immandra struggled, overcome with a surge of fear, adrenaline wildly pounding through her veins. Being brought to Matta Dora wasn't in her plans. Not like this. She felt Roxy's sharp claws through her clothes and realized the guards hadn't spotted the fox yet. They paid Kuiper little mind, unworried about so small a creature. Roxy crawled around to her back and she felt the wand nudged out of her belt. It clattered to the ground behind her.

Kuiper scrambled after Immandra and picked up the crooked wand. "Hey! You guys!"

The guards looked back with snarls. "Shut your trap, gnome, or find yourself our dinner."

"Been a long time since I've had roasted gnome. This one's a bit lean, but he'll be tasty all the same."

"I wouldn't give him the courtesy of a slit throat before putting him to the spit," the other guard stated.

Immandra uselessly struggled in their hold. "Please, no, you don't want him."

"You hush too, crone!"

Kuiper took a bold step forward and brandished the magical tool. "Release her! Be gone, you dog spawn from hell!"

Sparks flew from the wand. The guards released Immandra, their brows wrinkled in confusion. Both men stepped away and headed across the bridge, their gaits unsteady. Halfway across, they shifted. Wolves shook off the armor and loped the rest of the way across. The two darkly furred shapes disappeared across the stone dotted plain.

Kuiper stared after them, the wand held in his shaking hands.

"That was brilliant, Kuiper!" Immandra crouched down and carefully pried the wooden stick from his fingers. Then she embraced her small friend, holding him close until the trembles subsided. She knew too well the effect of Zyda's magic when used. It felt oily and hot. It felt frightening.

"C'mon," she said as she drew back and achingly rose to her feet. She took Kuiper by the hand and led the way through the gates.

"You didn't really mean it when you said you'd trade me, did you?"

"Of course not!"

They made it the rest of the way unharmed and unnoticed. Luck and fortune seemed to finally be on their side. It surprised Roxy, most of all, that they were able to reach the castle without any form of concealment. Of course, without the Doom Fliers soaring circles above the castle during the daylight hours, they had the advantage.

"We're here… now what?" Kuiper asked.

Immandra glanced at a small crack in the castle wall. The spaced gap in the mortar between the stone was too tiny for any human creature, and certainly too small for Kuiper. She plucked Roxy out of her pocket and gazed deep into the fox's eyes.

"I'm counting on you, Roxy. Please. Find Sian. Come back to me as soon as you find out anything," she told her friend.

"I'll be back as soon as I can," Roxy vowed.

"Take your time. I could use a moment of rest," Kuiper spoke up.

Roxy rolled her eyes and Immandra smiled weakly. The woman tenderly kissed the top of her pet's head and held her close.

"Thank you, Roxy. Thank you," she repeated for the second time. The fox sprang from her hold and scurried into the narrow fissure in the castle walls. Within moments, she was out of sight and traveling deep into Darknoor. Immandra prayed for her safe return.

Kuiper squinted at the same crack once Roxy was gone. He made a thoughtful "hm" noise to himself and inspected it. Crumbling bits of stone easily came away to widen the channel between the bricks. He brushed away more bits of rock and let a big grin overtake his wrinkled and haggard features. "This looks like as good a place as any to place that wizard's weird charm!"

"You're right."

Immandra thrust her hand into her pocket. She removed the mysterious charm Tarr Nettlewort gave her and turned it over and over in her hands in contemplation. Part of her was afraid that if she were to place it into the wall, it would bring the entire thing crumbling down with Roxy and Sian still inside.

"It's safe. Go ahead. It probably needs to be activated," Kuiper assured her. He helped her dig deeper into the small niche until they found stones missing from the walls. She felt around with her gnarled fingers and scraped at the disturbed mortar with her curved fingernails. The mystical talisman easily slipped inside. Kuiper patted the bits of rock and debris back into place.

Once they were done, it was practically impossible to tell that any meddling had occurred at all. Everything looked exactly as it had before the group's arrival.

"We'll see how it works soon." She wiped her hands against her skirt.

"Let's have a bite to eat while we wait. I'm starving."

"This is a terrible time to think of your belly, Kuiper."

"It's a terrible time to go into battle hungry! What if we have to fight for Sian?"

The thought had never occurred to Immandra. She'd always assumed that she'd rescue her husband, but she had naively lacked an idea of how to accomplish it. She frowned at the thought of fighting with Zyda's ancient body. "Okay," she agreed reluctantly.

Kuiper's beaklike nose twitched as he sniffed the air. She allowed him to lead her, depending on his heightened sense of smell and hunger. Surely enough, after merely a five minute walk down the cobbled street, Immandra caught a whiff of the same scent.

"That smells delicious." She leaned upon her staff, nearly out of breath from the effort to continue down the road. Old age was upon her and it was not kind.

"Mmm… it's fresh bread. Right over there."

They encountered a baker's shop with an open door. Fresh smells of mouthwatering treats drifted toward them on the breeze. Immandra felt her own belly rumble with hunger, reminding her of how poorly she'd eaten during their travels. Kuiper had the right idea in mind. Tarr's rations, while generous, had not been enough to last the entire duration of their travel.

She moved beyond the door and into the shop, blinking her eyes to adjust to the dimmer interior. A fat, sweaty individual stood behind the shop's counter, yellowing stains visible beneath the arms of his tunic. The baker seemed to have a taste for his own treats.

"What do you want?" he demanded. "I don't bake bread for beggars." The man scoffed and slammed the ball of dough onto the wooden surface to begin kneading it out. Flour dispersed into the air and clouded the small room. It was a cramped space, but the smells of pastries fresh from the oven enticed Immandra to stay.

"Have mercy on weary travelers," Kuiper entreated him. "We haven't eaten for days," he fibbed.

"That's your problem. My bread is only for those who can pay." The baker sneered at them, obviously without a lick of pity.

"We don't have money. We could help you clean the shop, or do some other work to earn our keep," Immandra spoke up quickly. She'd slave and mop his floors for a single apple tart. Clearly, she should have asked Ordalf for a couple of silver coins before he parted from her company.

"I don't need help. Now get out of here." He pointed toward the door with his heavy rolling pin. It looked as much a weapon as it did a tool.

Kuiper's face twisted into a scowl. "Perhaps you haven't noticed, sir, but there is a bunch of rats eating your fresh rolls. Serves you right then."

"Rats? Where?!" The man spun so hard he nearly wobbled over. His excessive rolls of fat jostled and bounced with the movement.

"Right over there," Kuiper told him, pointing. The baker hastily fled to the rear of the shop, brandishing his rolling pin.

Immandra followed the line indicated by the gnome's finger and peered into the back of the shop. She didn't see a single thing. Not that it mattered. The very moment that the baker turned his back to them, Kuiper swooped in and grabbed a roll in each hand from the tray. He hid them behind his back and innocently gazed around the shop.

Panting, the baker returned. He glowered at Kuiper. "I don't see anything."

"They were there only a moment ago. They must have gotten their fill and run away. Well, since you're far too greed to share with two unfortunate souls, we'll be taking our leave now." Immandra's skirts concealed Kuiper's wrongful acquisitions as they quickly made their way from the shop. The baker practically slammed the door behind them.

The two friends returned to the niche by the castle wall to enjoy their treats. The rolls were large and flaky, glazed with a thin, sweet icing that melted on Immandra's tongue. She hadn't enjoyed something so delicious since her time in Kaitan's temple. He'd generously fed her, but then again, so had Tarr. The wizard's breads were intended for travel and a lengthy journey. Hard and low in moisture content, they lasted quite a while at least, despite their unpalatable, bland taste.

"Perhaps we shouldn't have stolen these rolls," Immandra thought out loud, feeling a moment of guilt. She'd never stolen in all of her life. Of course, she hadn't been the one to lift the pieces of savory delight from the tray. Kuiper had done the dirty work for her.

"I haven't stolen them. It's a loan. We will pay him back when we can," Kuiper assured her. The gnome's devious expression made it difficult to believe him.

She chortled with genuine amusement while licking her fingers. It felt good to laugh. Today, they were going to rescue Sian. Soon she'd have her original body back too. Smiling at her friend, she asked, "Where did you learn to trick people like that?"

"Ideas come to me when the necessity arises."

"You're a smart gnome," she told him. She shook her head, but the smile never left her face. It was great to have trustworthy and loyal friends.

"Finally. Someone appreciates that."

Roxy sprang out of the crevice in the wall. Her quick little feet kicked up dust and grit. She panted and practically collapsed upon Immandra's lap. "Bad news, bad news!" she cried. "Oh, very bad news, Imma!"

"What is it?" Immandra looked down at her small friend. Many people didn't believe that foxes and animals were expressive, but Roxy's grim features terrified her.

"I don't know how to tell you, Imma…"

"Just tell me." *Please, don't take Sian from me.*

Please don't tell me that he's gone. Please, please, she internally begged.

"Matta Dora cast a spell upon Sian," Roxy began reluctantly. The small fox nervously swished her tail behind her and stepped down from Immandra's lap to pace. She looked acutely uncomfortable. "She succeeded and... he... he is her lover. He lives in her quarters and has for many days now. Zyda was right!"

Roxy's news struck her speechless. As much as she wanted to doubt her friend, a strange sense of understanding fell over her. Matta Dora was evil incarnate, and there were few things more evil than to manipulate another person's beloved into her bed against his will. Her Sian. Her poor Sian. Immandra's throat clenched and the air deflated from her lungs. She couldn't breathe and she couldn't see through the tears that filled her eyes.

Kuiper choked on a bit of roll. It took him a moment to cough up the small piece of flavorful bread. "Are you sure? It must be a mistake."

"There was no mistaking it, Kuiper."

"What am I to do now? All is lost," Immandra sobbed into her hands.

The gnome leapt to his feet. "It's not over."

Immandra furiously shook her head, tears trailing down her wrinkled cheeks. "I want to die. Look at me. I've done all of this, and I can't even hope to defeat her. She's stolen him."

"We can still win him back," Roxy said.

"Win him back? How?"

"Let me think. We would have to free him from the spell first," Roxy suggested. Her bright eyes seemed determined, but Immandra felt only failure in her heart until she thought of the people who had been slain by Matta Dora's hand. She felt defeated until she thought of Hessop and his noble sacrifice to see her to safety. She couldn't throw in the towel until she guaranteed the safety of Sinead from the evil Princess' control.

"You're right, Roxy. We'll fight. I must go to him and remind him that he's mine. This woman has no right to take him, no right to… to…" He was Matta Dora's lover. Another sob tore from her throat at the very thought of it. "She has no right to take him from me," she repeated firmly. A tremor ran through the castle and shook the foundations, punctuating her declaration. Dust and pieces of rock fell to the ground.

"Bless Tarr. The charm is doing its work," Kuiper said.

"Let's wait a few hours. After midnight, when everyone's asleep, I'll lead you to Sian."

Chapter Ten

THE RESCUE

Roxy led them to a quiet passageway in the dead of the night. No guards or servants traversed the halls. At least none they had seen.

"Show the way, Roxy," Immandra whispered.

"Remember, we must be careful," Roxy cautioned. "There are dragonlings and huge dogs guarding this place. Keep your voices low and your steps light."

"We'll be on guard. Let us find Sian now." Kuiper fidgeted slightly back and forth, from foot to foot, but his expression was determined.

They made their way through the castle silent as mice. Twice they ducked aside to hide from patrolling guards. The second time, the two armed soldiers passed barely inches away while the group hid behind a hanging tapestry and held their breaths.

"Dragonling!" Roxy hissed in warning. The fox paced worriedly. "This is the only passage up to Matta Dora's rooms. We will have to sneak by it."

"Sneak by a dragonlings?" Kuiper squeaked.

"It is asleep. If we move very slowly and make not a peep... we have a chance."

Immandra nodded. "Then we must try."

The room was round and not very large. The scaled, winged creature slept curled in the very center. Steam wafted from its nostrils with every exhaled breath. It's thick tail ended in sharp barbs and its four limbs were tipped with curved claws that appeared sharp enough to disembowel a man in a single swipe.

Immandra held her breath and carefully tiptoed along the rough wall of the room. Kuiper followed close behind her, clutching at her leg. Roxy perched on her shoulder and kept a watchful eye on the drowsing dragon.

The creature moved once and they all went still as stone. Immandra dared not to breathe, heart pounding as the dragonlings stretched and yawned. Its gaping mouth revealed a double row of serrated teeth. When it stilled again, they finished passing through. Their relief was short lived when they saw the iron gate at the end of the short passage.

"I think I can squeeze through." Immandra turned her body and wriggled through the bars. The fit was tight, made harder by Zyda's crooked frame, but she managed to ease her way through.

"My head... it's stuck." Kuiper fought to push himself through the gate.

"It's his ears. Blast them for being so large!" Roxy ran back and forth in worry and fear.

Immandra pulled and tugged on her friend, trying to yank him past the bars. In the distance she heard footsteps, which only added to her fear. They would all be caught.

"Go on without me then," Kuiper begged.

"Never! We've come this far, all of us, and I will *not* abandon you now."

Immandra tugged with all of her might. When it seemed the approaching footsteps were seconds away, Kuiper popped through the gate. She gathered her friend up in her arms and rushed after Roxy for cover in a small alcove behind a massive set of armor. They barely squeezed behind it when a trio of guards came around the bend and strode by on patrol.

For long moments they waited, catching their breaths and letting their pounding hearts settle.

"That was close," Roxy whispered. "Are you badly hurt Kuiper?"

"Only a little blood," he replied. His left ear had a raw scrape along its length. "I'll be fine."

"How much further is it to where they keep Sian?" Immandra asked. She applied a bandage to Kuiper's ear as best she could, tying a bit of cloth over the worst of it. Her stalwart friend grunted, but otherwise he made no sound in complaint.

"Come, follow me, we are almost there."

They crept from their hiding spot and continued up the hall. Roxy navigated the twisting corridors, finally leading them to a heavy wooden door. Intricate metal designs covered its surface.

"This is it."

Her heart pounded as she opened the door to reveal the inside of a lavish bedroom. She saw ruby red curtains, thick silk carpets, and a beautiful interior too rich to ever belong in her own home. She and Sian had modestly lived in a small three room cottage. Their entire home would have fit in the bedroom.

"Thank goodness," Roxy said. "He's alone."

Immandra cut her eyes toward the direction of the canopied bed. A man's familiar shape reclined amidst the plump pillows. His bare chest rose in the rhythmic, even pattern of deep sleep. With her heart in her throat, Immandra slowly approached him until she came to stand alongside the bed. Her fingers smoothed his sandy blond hair off of his forehead.

Initially, Sian sighed and leaned toward her tender touch. A drowsy groan parted his lips while he hung on the verge of consciousness, divided between sleep and waking. The appreciative reaction changed once his eyes blinked opened.

"Who are you?" Sian demanded. "Keep your sticky hands away from me."

Her husband jerked away from her, wearing a look of absolute revulsion on his face. He didn't recognize her. How could he when she had become the spitting image of Zyda?

Immandra reached for him again and blinked away tears. "Oh, Sian... You've changed so much. You've grown. I can't tell you how much I've missed you during all of this time."

"Get out of here before I call the guards."

"Don't you recognize me?" Of course he couldn't. Zyda's gray hair, wrinkled hands, and sagging skin bore no resemblance to the youthful wife he had left behind in Reindeer Keep Village. Her stomach twisted and her hands shook with anxiety. "

"Recognize you? I've never seen you before."

"She's your soul mate!" Kuiper cried.

"I have but one soul mate, and her name is Matta Dora. I don't know you." Sian's eyes darted to Kuiper and Roxy. "Who in the name of the Void are you?"

No... has he forgotten all of us? Immandra wondered in disbelief. She knew Matta Dora to be a capable and powerful dark sorceress, but she'd never expected to become lost to Sian's memory altogether.

"Don't you remember any of us!?" Roxy cried in frustration. "We came to rescue and take you home, you silly man! Tell him, Imma!"

"Even if you can't recognize my face, doesn't your heart tell you the truth?" Immandra asked him. She had to cling to her hopes and had to believe that Matta Dora wouldn't prevail. She sniffed and swiped her wrist across her tearful eyes.

"My heart tells me nothing. I have never met you in all of my life. This is my home and I need no rescue. I grow tired of your games." He grabbed Immandra by her rags and yanked. In old age, she'd become as light as dried twigs wrapped in tattered cloth. He easily yanked her forward and she banged her knee. Pain flared bright.

"Sian, please," she begged."

"Ehh! What a smell."

He shoved Immandra away from him. She lost her footing and tumbled to the stone mosaic floor. She'd never felt so defeated and broken in all of her life. Her tear-streaked face turned up to him, and she pleaded again. "Look, my love. This is the ring Queen Sibba gave me on our wedding day. She gifted the very same ring to you too. Isn't that proof enough?"

Sian seemed to recoil from the symbol of their

union. "What game is this?"

"He is blinded by a spell," Roxy whispered to Kuiper. "No matter what we say, he will not believe us."

"Then think of something Roxy. Look at poor Immandra! We must help her"

"I've an idea. Be ready."

Roxy rushed forward and darted between Sian's legs. In one swift movement, she turned, then sank her teeth into his leg. "You heartless, ungrateful, son of a... a skunk!" The little fox snarled up at the startled man. "You abusive little worm, beating up on a woman this way! You're nothing more than a slimy lizard." Roxy spit at Sian's feet. "Shame on you! How did Sinead give birth to one as revolting as you? Shame!"

"Er... Roxy, isn't that a bit too much?" Kuiper whispered over to her.

"Don't interrupt," the fox hissed back. She danced around Sian's ankles, snapping at his ankles while she continued her angry tirade. "You're a brainless, gutless scoundrel... that's what you are. An unspeakably sleazy and filthy scum. How dare you treat Immandra this way. How dare you betray your wife and one true love!"

Sian yelped and cursed, trying to evade each snap from the riled fox. Confusion swept across his strong features, uncertainty filling his blue eyes. "Why do you chastise me so? What crime have I committed to warrant such hateful words?"

"Look at what you have done to Immandra!"

Sian turned and rested his gaze upon the weeping woman on the floor. Immandra reached for him, but he didn't draw close enough for her to touch.

"This old crone, she is not Immandra."

"But she is!" Kuiper cried. "She has sacrificed all to find you!"

Sian warily offered Immandra a hand up to her feet. She looked up into his face, her tears coursing down her cheeks.

"Look into my eyes, Sian. My body may be changed, but my eyes are the same. Listen to your heart, I beg of you."

For a moment she thought Sian saw the truth of things. His blue eyes softened, and he lifted a hand to touch her cheek. Then his body shuddered and the shadows swam into his gaze again. His touch dropped away and he released her, taking a step back.

"No. It is impossible. I love... I love..." His brow furrowed and he struggled to speak. Suddenly his body relaxed, and a dreamy expression overtook his face. "I only love my mistress, Matta Dora. She is my world. My all. She is my every thought."

Cold washed over Immandra. The sensation of dread and pain left her frozen, unable to move.

"Your shock treatment didn't work, Roxy."

"It almost did. For a moment he looked torn..." Roxy whined. "What did I do wrong? They almost always snap back."

"Are you still here?" Sian seemed to notice the group again. "Go away or I'll call the guards. I won't ask again."

"I've lost him..." Immandra's words were barely a breath of sound. She heavily leaned on her staff, knees trembling. The idea of taking a single step seemed impossible. Sobs shook her fragile body and sorrow bent her shoulders.

"Immandra…" Roxy's voice drifted off. Without words of comfort, the small fox pressed up against Immandra's leg. Kuiper grasped the other and pressed his sorrowful face against her rags.

How did this happen? How did I come all this way only to lose him? Pain clutched her heart and made it hard to breathe, as if her chest were in a vice. The pressure built and built until she opened her mouth to speak. Instead, her voice came out in a shaky song, interrupted by her sobs.

> Will my love survive the trials?
> Is it strong enough to last?
> Ask the tree Ask the sky
> Ask whoever pass you--

Sian spun around. "Wait! How do you know this song, old woman?"

> Will my Sian still love me changed?
> Beauty gone and looking strange?
> Ask the lake
> Ask the grass
> Ask whoever you may pass.

> Will my love be still so strong
> To make fairy stone ring glow?
> Ask the f—

"Immandra?" Sian drowsily blinked and stepped closer. Both his hands lifted to cup her face and he drew her close, deeply staring into her eyes. "Bewilderment slowly widened his gaze. "Imma? Is it really you? Or is this a dream, another torture?

"It's me, Sian. It's me." Hope grew warm in her chest. It trembled through her entire body as her husband shook off the dregs of the spell and looked upon her in recognition.

"My little Immandra!" Sian wrapped his arms around her and lifted her into his embrace. "How could I ever have forgotten you?"

"The spell is broken!" Roxy leapt up in exhilaration. Her happy yips filled the room. Kuiper joined her, clapping and wiping at his tears alternatively.

"To know such love…"

"One day, Kuiper," Roxy reassured softly. "Even a grouch such as you can find such, I'll give you that."

The gnome gave the fox a bow. "Thank you. The same to you."

It warmed Immandra to see her friends getting along. Almost as much as Sian's arms. Despite the danger of their surroundings and her haggard appearance, she felt at peace.

Sian pulled back after a few moments, but kept his hands on her shoulders. Like her, his cheeks gleamed with tears. "It's not safe here. Matta Dora could return at any time. And my friends… the others who were captured, she holds them still in her dungeons."

"We must stop them. Both of them," Immandra insisted. "But we need to bring our friends home, no matter what. We can set Kuiper to the task?"

"Wh- what?"

Immandra turned and looked down at her small friend. "You are the bravest, cleverest gnome I know. If anyone can free our friends from their chains, it's you."

"We must destroy the Princess of Darkness. You wouldn't believe the things they do here. The torment that they cause other people who cross them. I have seen so many things, Imma. Horrible things," he confided in her.

When Immandra thought of what Roxy had told her, of Sian living alongside Matta Dora in her private chambers as her lover, her heart ached for him even more. Not only had her Sian seen terrible things, but he'd also been at the receiving end of them.

Immandra could no more hold him at fault for what happened during his captivity than she could fault the men kept in her dungeon. "They can crush us like ants. But it feels like the right thing to do."

"It does," Sian agreed. "We must at least try."

A strong shudder ran through the castle. Weakened by age and the difficult events of her journey, Immandra nearly collapsed to the floor. Sian saved her as she wobbled by, pulling her in against him firmly.

"What's that?" Small stones detached from the ceiling and rained to the floor. A couple plinked off of the top of Kuiper's bald dome.

"We ran into an old wizard who gave us a charm. He told us that it'll destroy the castle, so we planted it on our way here," Immandra told him.

"It's working rather nicely," Roxy commented.

Sian solemnly nodded his head and gazed toward the ceiling. A fine lattice network of fissure lines split across the stone surface. It didn't seem as if the charm would grant much time before it brought the castle to ruin.

"That's good, but Mizar and Matta Dora will escape if they see it coming. We have to stop them somehow.

We need to end them for good somehow so that they can't come back for revenge one day."

"Somehow! I like that word," Roxy chirped. "It leaves a lot of room for improvisation."

"How can we stand against them, my love?" Immandra asked him softly. She hated the sound of Zyda's voice from her lips.

Another stronger tremor ran through the walls of the castle. The foundation shook and rumbled until a wide crack slithered up the wall by the windows. Soon, the castle would be reduced to a pile of rubble.

Their only task, and most important mission, was to ensure that Matta Dora was inside when it happened.

"It's only a matter of time before these walls crumble," Kuiper said. "I wouldn't want to be here when it happens. I don't want *any* of us to be here when it happens," he added as an afterthought. "I guess that includes you too, Roxy."

"Gee, thanks."

Despite their seeming moments of friendship, it would have been unrealistic to expect her friends not to steal the occasional lighthearted jab at one another. Immandra smiled despite the tense situation. It felt good to smile and to have hope.

"We can't delay a moment longer," Immandra said as she took Sian's hand. The world around them groaned and shuddered, releasing another fine sprinkling of mortar and pebbles from above. Kuiper was right. Darknoor was no longer safe for them.

"They must know something's happening by now. Kuiper, go to the dungeon and free my friends. I'm sure you can do it."

"I believe in you," Immandra said to Kuiper. "We need all the help we can get now."

Kuiper quickly squeezed through one of the widening cracks in the wall and disappeared from Immandra's sight. The remaining three quickly hurried for the door as bits of stonework showered their shoulders and the tops of their heads. Nothing dangerous had been shook loose from the ceiling just yet, but it was only a matter of time.

We have to find her. We have to put an end to this madness, Immandra thought, her heart flooded with determination.

They found their exit cut off, blocked by a tall elven woman of dark skin. Her onyx-hued flesh contrasted against the silver coloring of her waist-length hair. She could have been considered beautiful under normal circumstances if not for the hateful grimace twisting her features into a terrifying expression. She easily blocked their way and strode forward, causing the trio to quickly step backwards toward the center of the room.

The intimidating presence before them could be only one person. Sian confirmed it in a tiny whisper, his frightened voice filling Immandra with dread. "Matta Dora."

"I thought I might save you a trip, my pet. Just where do you think you are going?"

The fear became determination. Sian's fingers tightened their hold on Immandra's hand. "You must let us go," he announced. He and Immandra exchanged helpless glances. He slightly moved before he took a protective stance, as if he meant to shield her with his own body.

"And if I don't?" Matta Dora asked. She sneered and

stepped forward, exuding a magical aura so strong that mystic winds kicked up the hemline of her velvet robes. Her silver strands of hair stirred behind her shoulders and her eyes gleamed.

"Then I'll have to kill you!" Sian declared. He released Immandra and dove for the wall where a spear hung as decoration. He whirled to face Matta Dora and drew back his arm. Immandra wanted nothing more than for him to pierce the witch's black heart and free them all from her torment.

"Kill me? You?! Don't make me laugh, puppet."

Immandra's desires weren't meant to be. Matta Dora raised a hand with her fingers outstretched. She uttered a single word. It was all that she needed. Sian screamed out in pain and collapsed to one knee, where he jerked as the spear suddenly tumbled from his lank grip. Wisps of smoke curled upward from his reddened fingertips and blisters rose from his flesh.

Heavier stones came loose as the next tremor shook the room. They noisily clattered to the ground and distracted Matta Dora from her victims. Alarmed, she darted her eyes toward the room as it rapidly began to fall into ruin.

"What is that?" she demanded. "What have you done to my castle?"

"It's your doom!"

"That is where you are greatly mistaken. It is your doom." Matta Dora whispered another word of power and directed her hands at Immandra in a sweeping gesture. Agony seemed to pervade every fiber of Immandra's being. It swarmed and surrounded her body in a cocoon of pain worse than the discomforts felt during her travel. The world around her grew larger and larger. The ceiling became a distant memory as she collapsed to her side, disoriented and confused.

"What did you do to Immandra! You monster," Sian cried from beside her.

Her husband had become a giant, towering above, long before he lurched to his feet and defiantly stood before their enemy. Even Roxy had become eye level with her, standing so close their whiskers touched.

Whiskers?

No... no, this can't be happening, Immandra thought in horrified dismay.

Matta Dora had transformed her into a rat.

"Eeeee!" Immandra shrieked in dismay.

"Come with me," Matta Dora demanded. She held out one hand outstretched toward Sian, a hunger shining in her dark eyes. In that moment, she appeared powerfully seductive, her power beyond anything that Immandra could possibly ever hope to overcome. "I've had enough of this foolishness. Her first mistake was to come here wearing the guise of my worst enemy."

"No," Sian refused. "I won't. I won't allow you to have power over me again."

A cold light flashed in the dark princess' eyes. Her voice rose again in another chant, lacing a magical spell that began to coalesce as illuminescent bonds around Sian's lean frame. They vanished without a visual trace, but the energy remained.

"No! I won't... I can't do this again. I won't look upon you and succumb to your vile magic again!" he declared. With what must have been the last traces of Sian's willpower, he tore free of one magical restraint and twisted the fairy ring on his finger. He closed his eyes and whispered, his plaintive entreaty reaching even Immandra's ears.

Zyda was wrong. Sian loved her, regardless of whether she occupied the body of an elderly woman or the shape of a rodent. He loved her, and he would do anything to keep her safe.

"I need your help, Mother. We are in great danger. All creatures, big and small, come to our aid."

Matta Dora chuckled and waved off his attempt to channel the forces of nature. "You amuse me, Sian. That's why I like you. This is Darknoor, the home of the Princess of Darkness. No aid will come to you here. No one will save you. You are mine again and your precious little fey will learn the taste of filth in my dungeons."

Sian ignored her and continued to concentrate, shutting his eyes against the appearance of her comely body. Immandra understood the reason for his closed eyes. Matta Dora's magic must have required line of sight. He had to see her! For as long as he didn't gaze upon her, he would be immune to the spell.

I need to help him, Immandra thought. Her beady rat eyes dropped to her left limb. She may have been a rat, but she still had tiny fingers. Surprisingly, the ring had shrank, adjusting to her new size. It gleamed as prettily on her rodent finger as it had upon her human hand. She quickly twisted it, using her teeth.

"I need your help, Mother. We are in great danger! All creatures, big and small, come to our aid!" Her heart overflowed with love and affection.

"I hear something!" Roxy cried. She took a protective stance above Immandra, using her slightly larger body to shield her friend.

Immandra heard it too. Her animalistic shape had given her sensitive hearing. A whisper of leathery wings announced that something was coming, and it was coming fast. Sian's call had been answered after all.

"Help is coming!" Immandra shouted. "Mother heard our prayers!"

Thousands of bats burst into the room, appearing from both ends of the corridor. They became a blanket in the air, their presence so thick that Immandra could barely see Matta Dora's livid features. They spilled into the bedchamber as a storm of flying rodents, fearlessly beating their membranous wings and furry bodies against the woman under their assault. They screeched and cried out, biting with their teeth.

"How dare you command my own subjects and turn them against me! You will pay for this! I will bleed you, I will rip your every vein from your body, flay the flesh from your skeleton!"

Words of power rose from her tongue as she pointed one slender finger with purpose. A flash of lightning tore through the room and laid waste to several bats. Their tiny bodies collapsed to the ground where they twitched and lay still. One bolt of lightning was not enough. Many flew sideways and dodged the assault, giving tiny cries of fear. It wasn't enough to deter them, for they appeared to be as numerous as they were determined.

"Hokatra wokatra sharaba doom!" A bright flash thrust the small creatures away, creating an impenetrable dome of power they were unable to cross. They collided against it multiple times as if they were striking glass.

It had the fortuitous effect of appearing to release

Sian from the clutches of the previous enchantment. The strain contorting his features faded.

"You cannot keep me here any longer, Matta Dora. I will be freed from you!"

"Ah, so you say, my dearest pet. But I will see you dead before I see you leave my possession. Ionadra, wonadra parada woom!" Matta Dora's voice rose in volume, gaining power with every spoken word. Her eyes flashed in the dim light of the bedroom, visible despite the cyclone of bats viciously attempting to invade her magical barrier. At the conclusion of the spell, the fallen rocks began to lift and swirl around Immandra, Sian, and Roxy. They formed a vortex of swirling energy and dangerous debris. A pebble nicked Sian's cheek, drawing blood, and another glanced off Immandra's ear. She cried out in pain, but Sian swept her from the ground and protectively held her against his body.

"Use the ring again, Sian!"

With Immandra clutched against his chest with his left hand, he used the fingers of his right to clutch his ring. "Spirits of stone, spirits of rock! Take her! Great Mother, hear our call!"

The ground beneath them rumbled again, but it had nothing to do with Tarr's sabotaging charm. Matta Dora's laughter became a blood-curling cry as the stone split. Startled, she stumbled to the left and the right to evade the crumbling effect of nature's might, but she tumbled into the precipice and the stone floor closed behind her. The only trace of what had occurred was a fine network of shatter cracks where she had fallen to her doom.

***

Kuiper hurried through the castle's dim, torch-lit corridors. The sources of light were kept spread apart, leaving long stretches of darkness in the halls. Kuiper hated the creepy feeling the place inspired. He felt as if eyes were on him around every bend. The distraction was so great he blindly ran forward through the next dark stretch, and promptly collided with something.

Two furred bodies turned and stared at the gnome. The large hounds bared their yellowed teeth and growled menacingly. A sharp bark from one echoed like thunder in the narrow space. The sound spurred Kuiper into movement. The little gnome spun around and ran as fast as his feet could carry him, the dogs in pursuit.

Adrenaline flooded through his veins and his lungs burned from exertion, but Kuiper didn't slow. He dashed to the right and heard the scrabble of claws behind him.

Faster, faster... I must be swift!

A barred gate loomed ahead. Kuiper put on a burst of speed. He wriggled through, the memory of his last attempt through a gate still fresh on his mind. His ear throbbed, but he dragged himself through with seconds to spare. The two dogs snarled and snapped their teeth, frothing at the mouth. But they could not reach him.

"Ha! Take that you stupid mutts," Kuiper crowed. He rubbed at his fresh bleeding ear then quickly shuffled off. Angry howls followed him.

Despite his harrowing encounter, Kuiper blundered forward into another spot of trouble. Over the barking hounds, he didn't hear the approach of booted feet. The gnome rounded a bend in the hall and came face to face with a guard squadron. Five sets of eyes narrowed in on him.

"You there! What are you doing here?" The guard's challenge filled Kuiper with dread.

"Um… I…"

"I asked you a question, gnome. State your name and business."

Kuiper stammered out his name. "I've been sent to check on the p-p-prisoners," he lied.

"Come closer and let me look at you."

"Please, sir. I'm in an awful hurry…"

The guard was not to be ignored and stepped forward menacingly. "I said step forward, knave, or I will run you through where you stand."

Panicked, Kuiper turned and ran. The demanding shouts of the guards followed him. A quick peek over his shoulder revealed they had all drawn their weapons. A crossbow bolt whizzed by his head.

Kuiper leapt to the left in what he thought was an alcove. The truth presented itself with vicious snarls and scalding plumes of smoke. A dragonling inhabited the chamber. With a startled cry, Kuiper backtracked into the main hall. His short stature allowed him to duck between the guards' legs and he raced back the way he had originally planned. The sudden change in direction granted him a few seconds head start while the guards turned themselves around.

It did him little good.

Another door barricaded the path, this one with a heavy padlock. A bolt hissed overhead and embedded itself in the thick wood. He was trapped, with nowhere else to flee.

"Nowhere for you to run now, gnome. Surrender!"

The castle shook. Stone rumbled and dust shook

down from above. The guards staggered. The wall behind Kuiper cracked and split. A hold opened up and the gnome dove inside. Sharp rock scraped his arms and face, tore at his clothes, but he valiantly pulled himself through. The escape took him past the door, where he heard the guards pounding.

Heart racing and chest heaving, Kuiper tore down the passage and nearly tumbled down the stairs at the end. The room below stank of sweat and refuse. Sputtering torches barely cast any good light to see by, which he used to his advantage. Kuiper crept forward through the dungeon, following a twisting series of passages. Rusted iron cells lined the walls, their moaning occupants coming from all walks of life. Some tried to reach for him through the bars. Others wept or snarled. Some begged for him to release them.

Kuiper hurried past them all, desperately seeking his friends. His feelings for the wretched prisoners ran from pity to disgust, fear and sorrow. There was no way to save them all. Not on his own at least.

He discovered Giber and Yorteze in a cramped cell at the back of the dungeon. Giber appeared the worst off. His sunken eyes darkly stood out in his dirty face and blood smeared his arms and ragged clothes. Yorteze's bark-like skin had dulled to an ashen gray, streaked with healthier browns. The branches of his crowned head had been snapped off.

"Pssst! C'mon boys, I'm here to get you out!"

"Kuiper? Is it really you?" Giber turned to look, disbelief shading his voice. "No... no, this is a trick. A cruel ploy."

"No, no, I promise it is me. Immandra, Roxy, and I

travelled here to free you all. Quick, where are the keys?"

"It smells like the gnome we know," Yorteze replied. He leaned towards the bars and drew in a deep breath. "Yes, he is of the hills. I smell the fairy child upon him. And the fox."

"See?" Kuiper stomped his foot and worriedly glanced back over his shoulder. "Now where are the keys?"

"Wait," Giber cried softly. "What of Sian? They took him."

Kuiper lifted his hands and made a calming gesture. "He's fine. Immandra and Roxy are with him. Matta Dora had him under a spell."

"Then he is where he would wish to be," Yorteze spoke. "As for us, the keys lie with the guards. You will have to sneak them."

"He's a gnome, Yort, he can't steal keys off a guard."

The sylvan looked down at the man and shook his head. "And yet he has made it this far. Let him try. He will either save us, or join us."

"I'll show you what a gnome can do, Giber Coltsfoot! Now, ah… where is the guard?"

"The next corridor over, to your left," Yorteze replied. "Go carefully."

With a puffed chest and his head held high, at least in his mind, Kuiper moved down the hall. Buzzing snores reached his ears before he peeked around the corner into the guard room. A table took up most of the small space, and the walls held an assortment of weapons. Some Kuiper couldn't identify, leading him to wonder what purpose they served.

Probably torture. Scary, evil fiends! I must get the key... but where? He darted his gaze about, grateful the two soldiers appeared to be dozing over the beer flagons. With quiet steps, Kuiper tiptoed in and scrambled up on a third chair. Keys hung on the wall between a chipped axe, in need of a good sharpening, and a wickedly sharp pair of daggers.

Noise behind him set his heart to pounding. Kuiper dived beneath the table seconds before one of the guards stirred. The man loudly belched, then slurped down more of his drink. Kuiper cowered in his hiding spot until silence ruled again.

I'll just take them all! No time to be choosey!

Quick as a whip, the gnome scampered back up on the chair and hastily plucked down the various keys. He counted ten in all, each one equally rusted and heavy in his grip. He bundled them all close to his chest and hastily withdrew, careful not to drop a single one.

"I'll be... he did it!" Giber cried softly.

"Of course I did! Now quickly, we need to find the right one." Kuiper dropped the keys by the door and his friends all grabbed one eagerly. They fumbled in turn with the large padlock on their cell door.

"Hurry up, hurry up," the gnome urged. "I hear footsteps!"

"Change of the guard," Yorteze told him in a grim tone. "Take the other keys, little gnome. Release the others and let us deal with the guard."

The door opened as the new guard came around the bend. He called out a warning, drew his blade, and charged. Yorteze swung his mighty arm and sent the guard hurling into the wall. His head struck the rock with a wet crunch and he dropped to the floor. The guard did not rise.

"Quickly, how many in the guardroom Kuiper?"

"Only two," Kuiper relayed. As bidden, he distributed the keys to the other prisoners to sort out on their own. "Both drowsing and drunk."

"Weapons?" Giber asked.

"More than plenty."

Giber and Yorteze hurried away. Low shouts and thuds echoed through the dungeon, then silence. Kuiper had no pity for the guards. He focused on releasing the others. The prisoners ranged in ages and races, but they all had one thing in common as far as Kuiper was concerned. None of them deserved to be left to Matta Dora and Mizar Thunderstone.

***

Sian ran through the corridors and burst into the great hall, Immandra carefully cradled in his hands. First his love was an old crone and now she was a rat. His heart couldn't bear the thought of what might happen to her next.

Sian hoped to find the hall empty, but it was quickly apparent that it was otherwise. Mizar Thunderstone and his officers all stood at the end of the hall. A shudder shook the ground, knocking Sian off-balance. Stone chunks fell from above and loudly crashed into the large chamber.

"My lord, we must evacuate immediately!" a grim soldier announced to Mizar. "An army comes from the forest and our forces are there to meet it, but the castle is falling down around us."

General Stern's appearance froze Sian on the spot, gripping his heart in absolute terror. Cold sweat broke over his brow while a recollection of many nighttime beatings swam to the forefront of his mind. The man resembled a brick wall and his fists equally struck as hard as one. Wide at the shoulder and thickly muscled in the middle, he used his power to abuse the captives held in Darknoor's dungeon. His cold cruelty matched his master's propensity for disbursing punishments upon his prisoners.

"He is correct. An unknown army appeared on the horizon. I have sent the Doom Fliers to dispatch them," General Stern said. "With the condition of the fortress, I advise you and the Princess to leave post in haste."

"Leave? Run?" Mizar's voice thundered across the hall, rivalling the sound of the falling stones. "Are you out of your mind, General? I do not run. Take your men and find the source of this disturbance. Destroy it!" Mizar leapt to his feet, a snarl on his face. "Use your head or what use have I for you? Now go!"

"Yes, my lord. At once."

Sian ducked behind a cracked pillar. The loud thump of his heart resounded in his head and sweat itched along his neck. "If only I could use this ring to make fairy fire."

"Try!" Immandra squeaked from his arms. Her sharp little claws clung to his shirt and lightly pricked at his skin beneath. Roxy trembled, perched on his shoulder.

Sian closed his eyes and held his hand over his heart. Immandra's whiskers tickled against his fingers.

He thought of his wife and focused on what he wanted – a wall of fire to defend them so they could run.

Through his eyelids light shimmered and danced, but the effort strained him too much. The magic curtain fell and fizzed out. Sian heaved out his held breath, eyes snapping open.

"I cannot do it. One must be of the fairy to manipulate such forces. It's too much for a mere human such as I."

"Mizar has seen us!" Immandra's tiny voice sounded more tiny and shrill with every word she spoke. Sian worried only squeaks would soon be left to her.

"Well, the lightshow gave us away," Roxy hopped down from Sian's shoulder, prepared to run.

"We must r--"

"Halt!" Mizar's voice cut Sian off. "You there, prisoner! Come here."

"Run!" Roxy urged, her fur fluffed up and her ears pressed back.

"I said come here, boy, or I will cause you pain you can only dream of."

Sian began to back away, panicked. Guards stood at the entrance where he had entered, but another doorway stood across the room. He grabbed Roxy and began to bolt for it. Barely halfway across the room, he fell back, the floor before him cracking open in a wide maw. Something crawled up from the depths and Sian retreated with an alarmed cry.

Matta Dora, bloodied and dirty, pulled herself from the gaping hole and rose to her feet. Malice gleamed in her eyes and fury contorted her face.

"Kill them!" she shrieked. "Kill them all at once.

Traitors! Deceivers! I will have their hearts on a plate!"

"Matta!" Mizar's shocked voice rang out. "Matta, what have they done to you?"

"Just do as I say and kill them!"

Chaos reigned. Mizar and his remaining guards rushed from the other side of the room. In the same instant, Kuiper appeared with Giber, Yorteze, and several prisoners. All of them bore a weapon.

"Sian! Sword!" Giber tossed a sheathed weapon to the man.

Sian caught the blade and quickly pulled it from its scabbard. Immandra and Roxy both scurried out of the way as the fighting commenced in earnest, hurrying to where Kuiper stood.

"What took you so long?" Roxy demanded.

"If you think freeing people from a dungeon is easy, do it yourself next time," Kuiper retorted. "Now quick you two, stand aside and watch me go!"

Kuiper rushed forward, wielding one of the razor sharp daggers from the dungeon. He slashed at ankles and stabbed knees, darting in and out of the fray. Sian briefly marveled at the small gnome.

Immandra and Roxy followed his example. They bit and clawed at their opponents. One rescued prisoner fell, but not before he took a guard down with him. Giber and Yorteze faced Matta Dora, dodging her spells or blocking them with a shield. Sian battled Mizar.

"Come round her back," Yorteze said in a low voice to Giber. The two men took cover behind a splintering pillar while lightning crackled around them. "I will keep her focus on me. You stab her from behind."

"I can't kill a lady."

"Then we are all doomed. She is no lady, Giber. She is the one responsible for your brother's death. For Furil. For the destruction of that village. She must be ended here."

Giber nodded, his face set in grim lines. They waited for the lightning to fade, then both rushed back towards the sorceress. Yorteze fought like a dervish. His natural claws, sharp as any blade, tore at Matta Dora's flesh and ruined clothes. With his fast moves, he kept the maddened woman focused on him. Giber took the opportunity and circled around under the pretense of engaging another soldier. He waited, breath held, until Matta Dora was fully exposed.

He charged with a yell, calling out his brother's name. "For Serlig!" His sword punctured through her back and out her front. The young man promptly released his blade and stumbled away, his breaths heaving and his eyes wide.

Matta Dora grasped at the blade, but found no grip on its slick surface. She didn't cry out, but rather stared around her in disbelief. The sorceress slumped to her knees then fell over to the floor, her body still. Dark blood soaked the stone beneath her.

"Ensure she is gone, Giber. I will help Sian." Yorteze wasted not a second. The sylvan creature spun around and charged the group surrounding Sian.

Giber cautiously knelt beside the body and reached out with a quaking hand. The moment his fingers touched Matta Dora's cold skin, she crumbled as if made of ash. The small bits wafted upwards and dispersed throughout the room, leaving nothing, but a small, dusty pile behind. A ruby pendant sparkled from the remains.

Matta Dora was truly finished.

With her death, all her recent spells shattered and lifted. Immandra returned to her prior shape, still bent in Zyda's body, but human and whole again. The lingering effects of Matta's devotion spell fell from Sian like water from a duck. His movements strengthened, no longer tethered by her magic.

Roxy barreled in to help, slamming her little body against a soldier's back legs. The man stumbled and tripped over the fox, stomping her tail in the process. Roxy yowled in pain and snapped her sharp teeth at his arm.

"Damned animal, I'll skin you and wear you for a hat!"

"Animal?" Roxy's voice rang with outrage. "He called me an animal!"

"Well, you are, aren't you?" Kuiper swung his knife at the attacker. The guard lifted the gnome up and shoved him against the wall.

Roxy took a running start and leapt up on the man's back, biting and clawing at his shoulders and head. He dropped Kuiper and cried out in pain. His sword clattered to the ground and he lifted both hands in an attempt to pluck Roxy free. Kuiper took advantage and charged his legs, knocking the soldier back to the floor.

"We make a good team," Roxy yipped with a foxy grin. The soldier's head struck the stone floor and he moved no more.

"Let's go help Sian," Kuiper urged. The two friends hurried across the room to join the rest of their friends. Mizar and his personal guards kept the group at bay, wearing them down and pushing them back.

Across the room, Immandra frantically searched her ragged clothes. Zyda's wand tumbled from the rumpled cloth, striking the floor with a clatter. She dipped down and picked it up with shaking hands.

The nearest soldier suffered her first magical assault. Immandra swished the wand and a green bolt shot from its tip. Her victim's skin hardened and turned brown, his arms became branches, and leaves sprouted from his fingertips and head. When the transformation was complete, an apple tree stood where a man once had. Immandra nodded in satisfaction.

"Keep it up, Imma!" Sian cried, parrying a thrust from another soldier.

The man facing Sian shrunk in size until he was no higher than Roxy, wide, and orange. She turned him into a pumpkin.

"That's the way to do it!" Kuiper cheered.

"Get Mizar, Imma! Get him now!" Roxy trilled.

Immandra turned her focus on the dreadful lord of Darknoor. The man fought like a demon, spinning through her friends like a whirlwind of destruction and chaos. Fury twisted his features. She pointed the wand at him and tuned out all else, praying for a miracle.

"Turn him into something harmless. Help us win this," she prayed softly. The wand vibrated in her hands and radiated an aura of cold. Chills swept from her fingers and Zyda's borrowed magic began to take action in the most unexpected way, igniting a sense of profound worry in Immandra's heart.

An acidic green bolt flew at Mizar. His shape twisted and warped, growing larger and larger by the second. The clothing and armor burst from his body, sending pieces of leather and chainmail in each direction. Red scales spread beneath his cracking skin and his face elongated into a reptilian snout with two twin slits at the end of the scaled nose. His rib cage expanded and broadened into a barrel shape as two tremendous appendages burst from his back. When it was done, a dragon stood where Mizar Thunderstone had been moments earlier, a terrifying substitute for an intimidating man.

The wand had betrayed her.

"Are you out of you mind?" Giber shrieked, stumbling back. "Change him into something else, Immandra!"

Dragon-Mizar roared and spat fire at the group. Sian's clothes caught aflame and he dropped to the hard ground, rolling across the floor to smother the inferno. Yorteze barely managed to dodge the next fiery blast.

"No, no, no! This is not what I wanted!" Immandra cried. She waved the wand again and it emitted fizzling sparks. "It's not working!"

Giber hacked at the dragon's thick, barbed tail, but his blade proved useless against the overlapping scales. Mizar slammed the man across the room with the muscled appendage and snapped his serrated teeth at the fighters.

"Immandra, the ring!" Kuiper called over. The gnome scrambled away from the much larger dragon. "Clear your mind and use the ring to control the wand!"

Clutching her hand over her heart, Immandra turned her gaze over the room. Everything seemed to slow and still, giving her a perfect picture of what was happening. Mizar and his last guard faced off against Sian, Giber, and Yorteze. Mizar's monstrous form took up nearly half the room and he used it to his advantage. Roxy and Kuiper, small as they were, continued to dart in and out around the last standing soldier. Their bravery knew no bounds.

People Immandra cared for and had come for stood at the brink of death. If Mizar wasn't stopped, she would lose them.

Her fear faded away, replaced with courage and certainty. She took the wand in her left hand and closed her eyes, calling on every ounce of love and devotion she felt for her people. She concentrated on what she felt for her friends and family.

The wand shook and protested in her hand, but warmth bloomed around her ring and steadied the magical instrument. She opened her eyes and raised the wand at dragon-Mizar. A blue glow surrounded him and shrunk the snarling creature down. Scales became fur. Instead of a dragon, a gray wolf snarled and bared his fangs at the group.

It wasn't a pumpkin or a tree, but it was better than a dragon. The wolf darted in to attack, but Kuiper threw a chunk of rock and struck his gray muzzle. Mizar snarled and turned his attention on the small gnome.

Sian drove his sword forward and struck wolf-Mizar in his chest, sinking the blade into his heart. A wooden bolt from Yorteze followed, driving in deeply.

Mizar Thunderstone whined and yelped. Then he fell. In death, his body shifted back to a man, but he lay motionless and still on the ground beside his sister's ashes.

As if proclaiming the deaths of its masters, the castle

trembled and violently shuddered around them. Stones crashed down from above and walls crumbled.

"Tarr's charm is working," Roxy yelled. "We need to get out of here or the whole place will crash in on us!"

Sian grabbed Immandra's hand. Giber picked up Roxy as Yorteze hefted Kuiper into his woody arms. The group turned and fled from the chamber, braving the quaking hallways. Dust and grit rained down from above, chunks of stone broke free and crashed down to the floors, but the group pressed forward.

Immandra cried out and stumbled, a rock catching her shoulder and knocking her off balance. Sian swept her up in his arms without ever breaking his stride.

"We're not going to make it!" Kuiper called out in fright.

"We must." Yorteze slapped a stone out of the air with his large hand. It shattered against the wall. Sunlight filtered in through the widening cracks.

Deep in the heart of Darknoor, a resounding explosion rocked the entire castle. The outer walls fell apart and flames rushed up the corridor. The blast lifted the group from their feet and hurled them forward through the air, all screaming.

Chapter Eleven

The Fall Of Darknoor

Gray streaks raced across the sky, smudged with shades of bruised violet and flushed gold. All the world stood still, from the silence of the trees to the absence of the winds. The unnatural hush blanketed the forest, as though waiting.

A crack from a snapped branch broke the quiet. Hoof beats duly thudded against the frozen ground and the leaves began to rustle overhead. From the morning mists, glints of metal flashed, and the first riders broke free into the yawning plain.

Junua rode at the head of the army, sitting tall on her copper steed. Darknoor's forces greeted their view, a massive black stain across the statue-dotted plain. Those who rode with her spread out down the tree line, a motley assortment, but all with the same goal in mind. The fearsome Horsetails on their muscled steeds comprised the core group around the sorceress, ready to attack on her word. They would spearhead their assault.

Behind them stood forty sylvan with living bows.

Nearly two-hundred men and women made up the bulk of their forces, armed with swords, shields, spears, maces, and sometimes pitchforks and common clubs. The common villagers willing to throw in their support had joined with any weapon at their disposal. Slingshot-wielding gnomes accompanied some of the riders, standing tall atop the withers of the war horses.

Five of Junua's sister witches rode with the army, spread throughout the ranks of armored men and women. They rode on giant stags without reins, leaving their hands free for casting spells. Three had been tasked with maintaining magical shields overhead to protect against the Doom Fliers. The other two and Junua prepared to wreak magical havoc on their opposition. All six of them carried battle-staves adorned with feathers and dyed bits of bone, a razor sharp blade attached to one end of the weapon.

"Great Mother," Junua murmured, sweeping her gaze across the battlefield. "Grant us strength and focus. Steady our blades, carry our arrows, and harden our defenses. Let us end this darkness."

The sorceress held her staff up into the air and brought down a blinding lightning bolt in the middle of the enemy ranks. Horses bolted and men fell back.

"For Sinead!"

"Sinead!" The echoing cry filled the air and carried over the thunder of hooves as they began their charge.

Above the gathering army, mutated winged creatures circled like vultures in the skies. Their numbers proved insufficient against the vast assault galloping toward Darknoor. Alone, the villages were easily overwhelmed by Matta Dora's forces, but united they were a force to be reckoned with. They rose against their old oppressors as the native townsfolk quickly quit the village surrounding the fortress, eager to escape the fate awaiting Darknoor.

Archers aimed their bows toward the Doom Fliers. "Fire!" the leading sylvan cried. Their arrows flew with incredible precision, striking the tender interior of their open mouths. One plummeted to the ground and struck the earth hard, where it lay thrashing until it choked to death on the arrow shaft penetrating its throat.

A second brilliant flash alerted their own aerial troops. The Mountain Fliers, led by Chappeewa, left their cover in the forest and took to the skies. They faced off against their warped brethren in a fierce overhead battle.

Metal clashed against metal, battle cries blended into a chaotic din, and discordant shrieks echoed across the wide heavens.

"Hold fast, proud warriors of Sinead!" Junua cried. "Show them that we are not to be underestimated!"

Fighting for their homes and loved ones lent strength to the people. Blacksmiths stood beside farmers and craftsmen, working as one against an enemy with far more skill. Mothers, fathers, sons, and daughters all came together to fight for their futures and freedom.

The sorceresses proved their worth time and time again, deflecting strikes from their allies and calling fire down on their enemies. Mountain Fliers scooped armed men into the air then dropped them from high above. The sylvan loosed volleys of arrows and rained destruction down on the opposition. Their living bows were far superior to any crafted by man.

Slowly, the tide of the battle turned in their favor.

"The castle shudders and breaks!" Chappeewa swooped down low on his Flier to pass the word. "People flood from its walls towards the hills."

"Any sign of our friends?" Junua asked. The weathered warrior only shook his head. "Their fate lies in the Mother's hands, then."

***

Immandra and her friends tumbled through the air then struck the hard ground with grunts and pained moans. Immandra and Sian landed in a tangle, but Kuiper protectively held Roxy in his arms. The two had become great friends at some point over the course of the journey. Giber and Yorteze rolled to a stop beside the other four at the base of the hill. Dust and grit covered them all head to toe, clinging against their unshaven faces and unkempt hair.

"Is anyone hurt?" Sian asked. He stood first without losing the opportunity to help Immandra to her feet as well. Months of captivity hadn't changed his gentlemanly manners. "Imma? You're holding your mouth."

"I lost a tooth. It's nothing," she reassured him, wiping at her bloodied lip.

"You're certain?" Sian asked worriedly. He gently cupped her face and inspected the damage.

"Better a lost tooth than a broken bone." She managed a small smile. "Everyone else?"

Giber flexed his arms and shook his head. Kuiper dusted a bit of dirt from Roxy's ears after he set her down.

"We are all alive, and all in one piece... more or

less," Yorteze said. He remained sitting on the cold ground, checking himself over. The long days of imprisonment had taken their toll at last, apparent in the dry exterior of his body and cracking bark skin.

"Sian, look…"

"Immandra pointed to the field and the battle waging across it. The two armies clashed. A final, deafening explosion at the castle brought the fighting to a sudden stop. Every face turned toward the crumbling edifice, shock and awe etched across their features.

"Your castle is gone, brought down by our might!" Junua's voice carried across the field. "Throw down your weapons now, for you have nothing left but your lives!"

The stately witch had no need to ask. Darknoor's forces began to throw down their weapons.

"Do not yield!" A deep voice boomed across the battlefield. A single figure emerged from the clouds of dust and smoke surrounding the fallen keep. General Stern stepped forward through the uncertain ranks. Men who lowered their weapons quickly raised them up again at his steely glare.

Immandra drew Zyda's wand and held it in a quivering grip, her white knuckled fingers skinned and scraped from the frantic escape.

"No, Imma. I can't let you face him in your condition." Sian placed himself between Immandra and the steel encased juggernaut known as General Stern. From afar, he resembled a giant towering among harmless peasants.

"My condition?" she demanded, more furious than anything.

Sian hesitated. "You don't know his power. Stern is a monster," he insisted. He attempted to hold her back with his hands to her shoulders, but the woman brushed his strong hands aside with newfound strength. She wouldn't be deterred.

"Stern should be the one to fear me," she told him, trembling with righteous fury. If Stern and his army were the only thing standing between Immandra and their freedom from Darknoor, then she would tear him apart with her bare hands. "I've been through too much to stop now." She had lost her body and a good friend along the way. The memory of Hessop and his courageous sacrifice brought tears to her eyes. Stern remained as the last symbol of Darknoor's oppression, the final obstacle to defeat for Hessop and for every other man or woman who fell as a result of Matta Dora's evil reign.

"What if Zyda's wand betrays you again?" Kuiper cried.

"It won't," Immandra stated grimly. Determination gleamed in her milky gaze, a hardened expression overtaking her weathered features. Sian heavily swallowed and stepped aside.

"Then I'll fight with you," he whispered. "I love you too much to let you face him alone."

"This army remains under my command," the General declared. "We will fight you all to the last. I will lead Darknoor anew and raze your pathetic villages to the ground."

"Brave words for a man whose Masters dare not show themselves. Your Mistress is dead, her magic broken."

Stern's hateful stare settled on Junua. "So long as I stand, Darknoor's enchantments hold."

"And yet you are outnumbered," Junua countered.

"Are you too cowardly to face me alone then?" the man taunted. "A duel to decide the fates of our armies. Who will oppose me as a real man?"

"I will!" Immandra cried out swiftly before any other could answer his call. "I will face you General Stern."

The man turned, a look of disbelief crawling over his face. His lips curled and then he laughed. "An old woman. Is this really the best you have?"

"I will stand with her." Sian pulled a sword from the dead fingers of a soldier lying amidst the rubble.

The General pointed his finger at Sian. "Don't make me laugh. I remember your face, boy, and I remember your cries." A cruel sneer turned his lips, accompanying his malicious chuckle. "Both sorts. I will take you and the old woman on. Let no one live to claim General Stern is not a fair man."

Sian faced the terrifying man head on. Their weapons clashed and emitted sparks. Without armor, Sian was faster, but open to attack. He used his mobility to his advantage, spinning aside from Stern's powerful, but weighted attacks. Immandra warily circled around their battle, aiming her spells at the behemoth. Most fizzled out against his armor and failed to move him.

"Stop thinking of it as Zyda's," Roxy yipped at her feet. "Use the magic in you, Imma. You can do it."

The magic in me... Immandra swapped the wand from her right hand to her left. *Use the magic in me... fairy magic...*

Initially, the wand resisted the exertion of her natural willpower. Immandra's continued focus won her a small success. A frosty mist spewed from the tip of the wand and billowed over the field. Soldiers shivered within their armor, the effect worsened by the heavy metal.

"That's it, Imma!" Roxy cried. "You can do it!"

Unhindered by any armor or protective covering, Sian weaved in and out with his quick reflexes. Stern's heavier battleax became a burden in the midst of combat. Sian's sword clanged off of the plate metal, but he barely maneuvered from the path of an axe strike meant to remove his head from his shoulders.

I need to do more. Stern will kill him if I can't!

No longer resisting her use, the wand readily answered in her hands. An emerald green glow spilled from the ring over her hand, wrapped in a twisting spiral up the wooden stick, and soared at General Stern in an impressive lance of light. Ice spread out from the point of impact, coating every armored inch. The General's skin paled and took on a bluish tinge.

Stern's defiant movements slowed to a crawl, too numbed from the extreme cold. His axe raised over his head, poised to cleave Sian into two.

He didn't have a chance. Sian's blade pierced Stern, the frozen general, through the chest. The force of the blow created a chain reaction, cracking the icy exterior and the frozen flesh beneath. His armor gave, weakened by the effect of Immandra's spell. Deep fissures formed around the protruding blade and created collateral cracks over the surface of his chainmail. Once Sian ripped the blade away, Stern's impressive armor shattered and fell to pieces. Moments later, the frozen general became a pile of rubble too.

"Yield now to us!" Giber cried, raising one sword above his head. "Yield now and we will allow you to keep your lives!"

A murmur of disbelief spread over the army. Eventually, the soldiers began to lower their weapons. Without their powerful general, few were willing to follow their leaders into death.

A loud cheer went up from the army of Sinead. For the first time in years, the skies were clear of Doom Fliers. The fearsome monstrosities were gone, never to return. Chappeewa and the other riders landed so they could join their fellows in rejoicing. Survivors from the destroyed keep wandered out of hiding to fall with tears and thanks on their saviors.

"Hurrah! We won! I can't believe it!" Sian rejoiced happily. With his arms around Immandra, he held her close and breathed in a sigh of relief. The nightmare was finally over.

Immandra leaned back within his embrace. Warmth flooded her spirits when their eyes met. It was as if Zyda's appearance weren't even there. He saw her down to her soul and loved her for the person inside. The witch was wrong. "Kiss me."

And then Sian hesitated. "Imma..." His arms left her waist so his hands could trace upward to rest upon her bony shoulders. She felt all skin and bones, her muscle wasted and spine curved into an impossibly crooked hump.

"You must kiss me, it's very important," Immandra whispered up to him.

The weight of four attentive gazes seemed heavier than ever. Giber and Yorteze watched while Kuiper and Roxy stood nearby in wait. All around them people rejoiced, but Immandra only had eyes for Sian.

"Why don't we wait?"

No. Zyda couldn't be right. She can't be, Immandra fretted. She feared for her true body, but most of all, the pain of rejection lanced through her heart. It didn't merely sting. It was excruciating. Tears blurred her vision and quickly streaked tracks down her wrinkled cheeks. She would forever become trapped in Zyda's body while the witch wore Immandra's true form.

"Imma, no, please, don't cry. It's nothing to do with your appearance," Sian quickly spoke up. He gently touched her face, albeit a little awkward. "It's just that… it feels like I'm kissing another woman. Like I'd be untrue to you."

"It's me in here, Sian."

"I know." He tenderly kissed her face without hesitation or reluctance. "I gave myself to you, body and soul, and I just can't bear to be intimate with… this hag's body," Sian confessed.

As he alleviated the ache in Immandra's heart, the others happily laughed. Roxy applauded and happily swished her tail while the men cheered.

Beyond Sian's shoulder, Immandra saw the field of statues gradually coming to life. Darknoor's conquests shook away the petrifying enchantments to reveal living, breathing figures. They were the brothers and sons captured over the many long years.

"Look! The others are awakening!" she cried. They moved slowly at first, as if doubting their own states of health. Gradually, the former victims knocked the dust and snow from their bodies and began to embrace one another in joy.

Among them, a single warrior stood out as strikingly familiar. Dool Sarsall raced toward his companions where he was drawn into welcoming hugs.

The quiet plain erupted with cheers and joyous cries, laughter and tears. Junua made her way to the group and broadly grinned at them all. She leapt from her horse and embraced her companions.

"But who is this?" she asked, turning her gaze on Immandra. "You look like one we know and abhor, but I can see goodness in you that Zyda does not possess."

"Plus that batty crone would never have fought for all these people," Kuiper added helpfully.

Junua laughed and bowed her head. "Well said, noble gnome."

"This is my Immandra, Junua," Sian boasted proudly. He took her hand in his and raised it to his lips. "And it would seem she and I have one more battle left to fight."

***

Melting frost trickled down the barren branches of trees surrounding Zyda's decrepit hut. It quickly became apparent the old woman in her new and youthful body hadn't expected them to return. She wore a flattering dress in soft green velvet. The long sleeves nearly spilled into the cauldron's contents. For Immandra, it was an out of body experience that traced a shiver down her spine. She walked faster, eager to be reunited with her true form.

"Hello there!" Sian called loudly as they approached. "We came to claim what's ours." He wore a big, friendly smile on his handsome face, but it didn't seem diminished at all by his hardships. Her Sian was back again, and it was as if seeing her true body had rejuvenated his spirit too.

"Ah, it's you." Zyda turned to face them, wearing disappointment on her lovely face.

Immandra smiled back at her and nodded. "I've done my part. I'd like my body back, if you don't mind."

Zyda indignantly sniffed and folded her arms against her chest. No. Immandra's chest. It was all wrong to see her body in the control of another person. "I do mind," the witch said. "My tooth?"

"Tooth?" Immandra blinked and raised a hand to her mouth. Zyda may have been old, but she hadn't been a toothless crone. She'd had each of her original teeth, yellowed and crooked, but whole and present. Now a single tooth was missing in the very front. It formed a wide, clearly noticeable gap.

"My tooth," Zyda repeated. "What did you do with my tooth?"

"I lost it during one of the trials. I'm sorry about that."

"Sorry?" The witch became livid, turning red in the face and refusing to budge on the spot. "I took care of your body. Do you think that a simple apology will be enough to repay what you've done to my body? Look. Not a scratch!" Zyda declared, gesturing toward Immandra's flawless body. "Yet you have lost... my... tooth!"

"I said I was sorry, Zyda. What else can I do?"

230

"You can keep my body. I don't take damaged goods. The deal is off." Zyda whirled on the spot and stalked toward her hut, leaving the group behind.

"What?!" Roxy and Kuiper cried in confusion.

"That isn't fair!" Immandra said. Tears stung her eyes and blurred her vision. The very thought of living the rest of her life in Zyda's body made her ill. She couldn't imagine forcing Sian to endure every day of their marriage as the husband to an old hag. Suddenly, she thought of the many things she would lose if she were to remain as Zyda. A chance to grow old together. The chance to have children. Zyda had long surpassed the prime age of motherhood, and she highly doubted Sian could bear to see beyond her hunched spine, wrinkled skin, liver spots and thinning white hair.

"Wait a minute!" Sian's protests jerked her out of her tearful revelations. "I won't let this happen." He stalked forward but Dool reached out to hold him by the shoulder.

"She's a witch," he whispered. "Are you sure that you wish to do this?"

"I won't allow her to cheat my Imma. She deserves to have her body back after all she's suffered," Sian said. He shook off his friends hand and continued forward boldly. "You and I have something to speak about, Zyda. I want her body back."

"What you want is of no concern to me," Zyda said petulantly. "She lost my tooth. She can keep the body."

Sian glanced back at Immandra thoughtfully. When he turned to face Zyda in her false body, his features had become hard as stone. Immandra had never seen him so serious in all of her life and time of knowing him.

Something about his trials in Matta Dora's castle had changed him.

"I wouldn't do that if I were you, Zyda. Fairy Queen Sibba may get very upset about a human stealing the body of a girl who is fairy born. Our Lady is your superior in magic, isn't she? I suppose she even has the ability to take away your powers."

"That's blackmail!" Zyda shouted. The outrage rose in her voice.

"Some people might call it that, but I'd call it a fair trade. Immandra's body in exchange for your magic. But I suppose this means that isn't a trade you're willing to make. Shall we talk then?"

Zyda suddenly became incredibly receptive to conversation.

***

Less than a week later, Sian, Immandra, Roxy, Kuiper, and the other surviving adventurers made their safe return to the Raindeer village plaza. Their horses whinnied in joyful anticipation of a warm stable and sweet oats. The enthused group of eager soldiers spurred their mounts and gave victorious whoops.

Immandra grinned from her place behind Sian. She rode with her arms snugly wrapped around his waist, her face buried against the back of his shoulder. A sense of belonging permeated every fiber of her being. How had she ever considered the fairy knight's offer? Reindeer Keep Village had become more than home, and she never wished to leave again.

Villagers welcomed them with cheers and joyful

cries. Some ran from cottage to cottage, notifying neighbors of their victorious return. There were so many tearful faces gathering at the village center that Immandra lost count. She hadn't felt so much happiness since the day Sian took her as his wife in the very same village square.

"Immandra! Blessed Mother, child, we worried when you disappeared." Druid Thorn rushed to meet them. His beaded headpiece had fallen askew in the rush and sat crooked atop his head. It slid to the left and nearly toppled down to the ground. "Junua told us of the ambush. We feared the worst for you boys. Where is she? How did it go?"

"Mission accomplished, Venerable One. Darknoor is but a crumbling mountain of stone," Sian informed him proudly. He squeezed Immandra close with one arm around her shoulders. She happily turned her head to his his cheek and hugged him in return. "Our warriors should be home any day now I reckon. Junua and Chappeewa wanted to ensure no other dangers lurked in Darknoor's ruins."

"Well done, my children. Well done. Now the great separation is no longer needed. Sinead will be a happy place once more," Druid Thorn said. He broadly grinned at the group.

"Everything will be as it was before," Sian agreed.

"You've found each other again, I see," Druid Thorn said, gesturing with a hand toward Immandra and Sian.

"I found her," Sian bragged, grinning. In the week since their reunion, he had slowly emerged from his tortured shell and begun to display some of the fun-loving and humorous traits Immandra knew best.

"Just a minute, Sian. It was I who found you!"

The group laughed. Amidst the laughter, there were tears and embraces of genuine relief and joy. Everyone didn't safely return from their adventure and they would sorely miss the fallen. Druid Thorn threw a celebration to honor those lost to the evil of Matta Dora. Giber mourned the death of his brother, and yet he was able live while knowing his twin hadn't died in vain.

All around them, the snow had begun to melt and reveal patches of lush green grass. By nightfall, every member of Reindeer Keep Village worked together to bring happiness to their returning champions. The men spent that early evening in the midst of a great hunt and by nightfall, had supplied everyone with the makings of a wonderful feast. The women of the village put together a grand dinner worthy of a dozen kings. The minstrels and bards stroked their harps, sang, and played wind instruments.

Children laughed and played, running with magical sparklers that released an array of colorful effects into the evening air.

It's so good to be home, Immandra thought as she leaned against Sian. She let her face rest against his throat, her eyes closed and long lashes tickling his skin. It felt so good to hug him and to think of the future. Childish laughter surrounded them and she could think of nothing more than to look forward to when their own home was filled with the sounds of youthful giggles.

The various sylvan creatures, who dwelled in the forest, performed tricks of agility and somersaults. The spry beings leapt and danced, twirled and flipped through the air. Villagers clapped and cheered them on.

From the corner of her eye, Immandra saw Kaitan Speedwell limping toward the village plaza. Lady Sibba intercepted him and stepped between them. Her stern expression made even Immandra flinch.

"Don't you dare to speak one of your ill omens of misfortune? We've had enough of your bad influence, Kaitan Speedwell. Can you not see that we are celebrating? It is well-deserved and these young people have earned their night of joy." Her eyes shone like blue sapphires in the night. Immandra felt a mere hint of Lady Sibba's power. She stood in awe of it, staring all the while.

"I was going to congratulate them. That's all."

Lady Sibba and Kaitan faced one another for a time that seemed to last infinitely. Tension spread through the nearest villagers and onlookers who were witness to the scene.

Immandra knew better. During her journey, she saw a softer, kinder side to Kaitan. She didn't think that he intended to do anything wrong at all. "I... I believe him, Lady Sibba."

The queen nodded her head and stepped from Kaitan's path. She watched him no less intently once he moved past her towards the couple.

Kaitan spoke the truth. For once, he came not to bear any omens of death or dark visions. He brought good tidings and words of peace. He respectfully bowed to Immandra and Sian.

"A lifetime of happiness and many years of joy to you. May you live in peace forever more," Kaitan said as they bowed to him in return. "For you, Immandra, I see a life surrounded by loved ones."

"Thank you, Kaitan.

At the height of the celebration, Sian and Immandra parted from the group and ran to the hawoo tree. They wanted to personally speak to him after ending their long adventure.

"I'm happy for you, my children. A little joy is good for an old tree like me," said the hawoo tree.

"Oh, Grandfather! It's so good to be back and to see happy faces one more time!" Immandra cried as she threw her arms around the hawoo tree. Her tears trickled down his cool exterior bark after she kissed his trunk.

"Love always wins at the end... I always had my faith in you," the venerable old tree said. His voice proudly rumbled, filled with renewed strength. The return of spring had brought back his power.

As Immandra drew back from hugging the tree, she glanced back to see the approach of Lady Sibba. She quickly dipped down into a respectful curtsy. "Lady Sibba."

"Sian and Immandra, I wished to give my congratulations to you personally. I am glad to see you have made a safe return. I always had faith in you."

"You knew that we would?" Immandra questioned. She uncertainly gazed at the queen.

"Of course I did. You passed the test, my children. You returned magic to the world as I knew you would."

Tears welled in Immandra's eyes. She impulsively threw her arms around Lady Sibba and rejoiced when the queen hugged her in return. They stood that way together for a time as Sian stood nearby with a warm smile on his face. The villagers danced and sang in the background, filling the night air with the sounds of merriment and celebration.

All was right with the world, and peace was restored to Sinead.

Fill your heart with love.
For love is and always will be
The strongest weapon for eternity.

Fill your heart with love
Make your world a better place
Bringing peace to the human race.

Fill your heart with love
Every trial in life is a test
Learn to love and win the rest.

Fill your heart with love
Bring back magic to your life
Wonders that'll never die.

Fill your heart with love
And listen to the waters sing
Talk with the trees
Dance with the wind.